BOA
EDITIONS LTD

THIS NEW &
POISONOUS AIR

THIS NEW & POISONOUS AIR

Stories by

ADAM McOMBER

AMERICAN READER SERIES, NO. 15

BOA Editions, Ltd. ✎ Rochester, NY ✎ 2011

First Edition
11 12 13 14 7 6 5 4 3 2 1

For information about permission to reuse any material from this book
please contact The Permissions Company at www.permissionscompany.
com or e-mail permdude@eclipse.net.

Publications by BOA Editions, Ltd.—a not-for-profit corporation under
section 501 (c) (3) of the United States Internal Revenue Code—are made
possible with funds from a variety of sources, including public funds from
the New York State Council on the Arts, a state agency; the Literature Pro-
gram of the National Endowment for the Arts; the County of Monroe, NY;
the Lannan Foundation for support of the Lannan Translations Selection
Series; the Sonia Raiziss Giop Charitable Foundation; the Mary S. Mulligan
Charitable Trust; the Rochester Area Community Foundation; the Arts &
Cultural Council for Greater Rochester; the Steeple-Jack Fund; the Ames-
Amzalak Memorial Trust in memory of Henry Ames, Semon Amzalak and
Dan Amzalak; and contributions from many individuals nationwide. See
Colophon on page 180 for special individual acknowledgments.

Cover Design: Sandy Knight
Cover Art: "Miss Doro, No. 2." c. 1902. Burr McIntosh Studio
Interior Design and Composition: Richard Foerster
Manufacturing: McNaughton & Gunn
BOA Logo: Mirko

Library of Congress Cataloging-in-Publication Data

McOmber, Adam.
This new and poisonous air : stories / by Adam McOmber. — 1st ed.
    p. cm.
ISBN 978-1-934414-51-4 (alk. paper)
I. Title.
PS3613.C58645T48 2011
813'.6—dc22
                    2010029669

NATIONAL
ENDOWMENT
FOR THE ARTS
─────────
A great nation
deserves great art.

BOA Editions, Ltd.
250 North Goodman Street, Suite 306
Rochester, NY 14607
www.boaeditions.org
A. Poulin, Jr., Founder (1938–1996)

State of the Arts

NYSCA

Contents

The Automatic Garden

AT A LATE AGE, Thomas Francini, the engineer responsible for many of the grand fountains at Versailles and infamous for his will to control, married the sixteen-year-old daughter of the Compte de Frontenac, a pristine child whom he dressed in taffy-colored velvets and ribbons and paraded through the Villa di Pratolino near Florence. Francini bought his young wife what she pleased from torch-lit shops, and what she could not find, he invented for her, producing a variety of curious wind-ups. She possessed a clock in the shape of an oversized parakeet with pearl eyes and jade plumage, set to trill at the lunch and dinner hour. There was also a small silver man that cried like a newborn until held, at which point he would grow intensely warm to the touch. Finally, the pinnacle of her collection, a miniature Madonna that swung open to reveal a trinity—the fierce and stoic God and fiery dove of the Holy Ghost ready to be birthed alongside the infant Christ.

When asked about her husband, the child bride, called Florette, said it was as if the Lord had sent his kindest angel to care for her and keep her heart in a treasury box, safe from all those who would harm it. She could never be bruised or pierced with the great inventor at her side. But soon she learned that even Francini could not stop time and the persistence of disease. Plague blossoms spread on the skin of her throat, and he was reduced to sitting at her bedside, wiping sores with swabs until the organic machinery of Florette's heart and lungs had stilled. He declared he would not marry again and wore a musical locket around his neck that held the child's portrait and played strains of "Come, Heavy Sleep" at intervals timed to match those that sounded inside Florette's own mechanical coffin. Soon after the girl's funeral, Francini purchased a portion of land and announced he would construct his final great invention there, a monument to sorrow for everyone to see—the automatic garden at Saint-Germaine-en-Laye.

The writings of Clodio Sévat, Vicar Emeritus and servant to the Dauphin, give us a brief glimpse of Francini's garden and echo the general anxiety of seventeenth century French and Italian aristocracy concerning that place: "Though it has been nearly a month since my pilgrimage to Saint-Germaine-en-Laye, I still cannot wipe the yellow-stained eyes of Thomas Francini's metal men and beasts from my memory, nor can I forget the sight of Francini himself stalking through his field of glass flowers like some devil, dragging what appeared to be a common garden hoe behind. Does Francini believe that God's good works should be made again, and that *he*, however noble an engineer, can improve upon them? And what soul motivates these new creatures? He assures us it is mere water and steam, but, dear reader, I tell you it is more than that."

Gladly, not all travelers were as brief as the Vicar Emeritus, lest the automatic garden, which burned to the ground nearly a year after its opening, might have been lost entirely to time. "Maestro Francini's water- and steam-powered automata," wrote the Duchess of Langres in her private journal after a trip to the garden, "are of a new and unexpected breed. I was warned by my companion that these false creatures might disturb me with their preternatural resemblances to life, but I instead found myself intrigued. Their ability to exude what appeared as emotion was startling, yes, but not frightening. Never in my life did I think I would see a tiger ravaged by *sadness* crouching in the underbrush and looking at me with amber glass eyes, or Poseidon himself, crying tears into the very ocean that he rules—tears that were then swallowed by a thick and toothy monster who lives in the ocean's depths. I was moved to call for an interview with Maestro Francini, wishing to enquire about the labyrinthine secrets of his inventions. And yet despite my status and the fact that I had attended the funeral of his bride, Florette, I was rebuked by what appeared to be a page in a red tunic who told me that the Master was frail and no longer tolerated audiences. It was only after the page's retreat into a forest of metallic pines that my companion, characteristically droll, asked whether or not I'd caught the sun glinting oddly off the young man's skin or whether I'd seen the glassiness in his eyes.

"I drew my wrap closer and begged my friend to assure me he was not implying that the page had been some advanced version of Francini's moving statuary. He replied with a laugh, saying he'd only been trying to give me chills, but by the time I'd reached the garden's third terrace, I did not need such humor to provide tremors. It was there that I saw what I can only describe as a 'dragon' rising from a stone basin, only to be slain by a lifelike knight in white armor who descended from the columned ceiling on a golden rope. The dragon's blood was as red and real as my own, yet it spread across the flagstones in delicate calligraphy as if sketched by an artist's hand. I was forced to ask my friend to find a bench on which I could gather my wits. 'We shouldn't have come here, Duchess,' he said, but I replied that I was glad we'd come, despite the effect. Francini's automatic garden showed me that a certain sickness—a questioning of one's world—could serve as a kind of enlightenment."

Like the automatic garden, the answer to whether the death of Francini's wife, Florette, had truly given rise to his monument of sorrow is largely lost to history. Francini's motivation for his final invention was a topic of debate in fashionable circles, and many argued that there was more to the inventor's grief than the death of poor, simple Florette. Gossip about such details was often named as the cause of the inventor's self-imposed exile to Saint-Germaine-en-Laye and his distancing himself from the aristocracy. It was not Florette who'd shamed him, after all, but the prior object of his passions who had made for a near public embarrassment and perhaps even venial sin.

Antonio Cornazzano had been a danseur and general actor of the Florentine stage who'd met the great engineer during the period when Francini was commissioned to build a revolving set for *La Ballet de La Deliverance de Renaud*. Francini, who could then still be called a young man, adored the danseur, and that affection was apparently reciprocated. The two were often seen huddled in dimly-lit taverns of Florence over a candle and a serving of black ale, discussing topics in such hushed voices that no one else could hear. Despite the apparent gravity of these discussions, Francini and Cornazzano sometimes burst into hearty laughter, and tavern patrons reported an unnatural magnetism between the two men. There were even rumors of sorcery, though André Félibien, court historian to Louis XIV, dismisses such conjecture as peasant talk. "Simply stated," he writes, "Thomas Francini and Antonio Cornazzano behaved as artists will, and though such behavior seems, at times, against nature, we must learn to accept and make do if the theater is to persist."

Francini's revolving stage set for the ballet was said to be a marvel—a replica of the city of Florence itself. And the ninety-two dancers and singers employed to move through the mock streets, bedrooms and common houses did so in an exhaustive display of "city-life" which also encompassed a *spiritual dimension*, as the upper parts of the central stage contained sets for the unmovable Empyrean of the Heaven. Masked angels and demons pulled silken ropes connected to doorways that affected the lives of the human dancers. Cornazzano acted as choreographer for the production and worked closely with Francini to create what many called a "threatening sense of fantasy."

The emotion between dark-featured Francini and agile Cornazzano developed a volatile irrepressibility. They could not contain themselves even when they worked with the dancers, and were often seen erupting into laughter and pulling each other out into the alley behind the theater to calm themselves with sobering talk. It was only when they lurched back to Francini's rented villa one night after drinking and were set upon by a band of Florentine locals and dashed to the flagstones that the two men became more cautious.

When precisely they decided to begin living inside of Francini's revolving set for the ballet, we do not know, but a number of sources document that Francini, who'd already made his fortune at Versailles, started stocking the taverns and shops of the set with actual goods and even hired out-of-work ballerinas to act as barmaids and shop keeps. He and Cornazzano lived privately on the stage, setting up house each night after the performance ended, enjoying that false city as they had previously enjoyed the actual streets of Florence. There were taverns in which the two could drink black ale by candlelight without the interruption of noisy patrons, and there was a library filled with fake books. Actual texts proved unnecessary because Francini could recite portions of *Le Morte Darthur* as well as *Gargantua and Pantegruel* by heart. At times, the two men climbed into the Heavenly domain, lit the wicks of the stars, and floated through the Empyrean on Francini's cleverly concealed wooden pallets.

A ballerina managed to steal a letter that Francini had left for Cornazzano on a pillow in one of the small apartments. The letter ended with a line that became popular in Florence as fashionable blasphemy: "I do not love God, my darling, 'Tonio. For what is God when there is you?" Cornazzano's response to those words remains in ellipsis. The content of the young man's heart is largely unknown. It is only years later that we hear from him in his own words. By then, he had married and seen the birth of three children with his wife, Marie, and together they owned a small theater in Charleville. Cornazzano wrote his thoughts in a sturdy leather diary which he then concealed in one of the walls of his home. In recent times, the diary has surfaced, and while it provides an uncomfortable end to the story of the two men, it gives evocative details of the automatic garden itself, which Cornazzano was invited to visit by the great inventor a month before fire consumed it.

Cornazzano begins the journal with intimations of the falling out between Francini and him years before.

They'd apparently abandoned their home in the revolving set long before the *Ballet de Renaud* had closed. "It has been years," he writes in his careful yet unschooled hand, "and I wonder if I am being overly cautious or cruel by suggesting that we meet at the garden itself rather than at Francini's home. I do not want to recall our *privacies* or the invented world we shared. It wasn't merely the stage—our fake city. We invented places in our minds, as well, that we could slip off to even in a crowd. I remember what Thomas said to me—that two men living together is in itself a kind of invention, a household of dream furniture and shadow servants. Is it wrong that I do not want to even come close to this dream again? How would I explain such a thing to my dear Marie or to my children, the eldest of whom is almost the age of Thomas's own bizarre deceased bride. By coming to the automatic garden, I hope to appease him, so that his letters will stop. I admit I am nervous to see what he calls his 'great defiance,' his palace against the day."

Cornazzano writes that he was greeted at the garden's columned gate by a page draped in a cloak dyed the color of saffron and told that Master Francini was unwell and sent his apologies for not being able to join Cornazzano on the tour. This came as quite a surprise to Cornazzano who'd believed the entire reason for this trip was so that Francini could see him again and perhaps persuade him that this place was like the other fantasy in which they'd lived—a new set for a fresh and dangerous ballet.

He attempted to beg off, saying that he was a busy man with a theater to run and did not have time to walk the garden if Francini could not be bothered to escort him, but the page became insistent, grabbing Cornazzano's arm and pulling him into the garden toward the forest of the gods. "Please, Monsieur. Master will be miserable if you don't at least give me some word of praise for his inventions." Finally Cornazzano conceded to take a short walk through the place, writing, "The page's hand was cold—not like a dead man, but like one who has never lived. I feared disagreement, so I allowed myself to be led." The walk turned into a game of mad circling through the garden's multiple levels and in the dim light of a forest path, the page disappeared, and Cornazzano was left alone with Francini's glowering mechanicals.

He became intrigued by a bed of glass chrysanthemums—a flower of the orient, rarely seen in France. The stem of the mechanical chrysanthemum was made of green copper with sharp-edged leaves protruding, and the petals of the flower itself were crafted from thin pieces of stained glass. Inside the stem was what appeared to be a small flame of the sort one finds in lanterns which was given oxygen at regular intervals, causing the chrysanthemum to pulse with a light that suggested the process of blooming. The brightening of the flower was subtle, nearly imperceptible, and Cornazzano writes that even after studying the chrysanthemum for a few minutes, he was hard-pressed to say whether it was growing brighter or dimmer. The light seemed to exist somewhere inside of his own body, in fact, a warmth in his core. "The mechanical chrysanthemum causes a momentary dizziness with its warmth," he adds, "a sensation that is not altogether unpleasant."

So entranced, Cornazzano did not recognize the approach of the figure in black, and when he caught his first glimpse of it standing at the stony edge of the garden path, he did not fully comprehend what he saw. He attests instead to being startled as one can be startled by an unexpected mirror hanging at the end of a gallery. The figure that stood in the grass and watched him was not an obvious automaton. Unlike the moving statue of Poseidon who wept into his miniature ocean, or the huntress, Diana, who drew her bowstring in the dark forest, this figure, had a versatile range of movement. It was able to crouch, then stand, and then to caper there at the edge of the path, as if begging for Cornazzano's approach.

Our chronicler likens the figure to one of the dancing fauns in the garden's Doric gallery, but man-sized and wearing a garment that looked like a merchant's robe with a wide lace ruff around its neck. The collar was crenulated and gave the appearance that the automaton's head, bearing its pale and almost luminous face, was displayed on a black plate. Its mouth was open in what could not be called a smile, and so surprising was the creature that Cornazzano did not at first recognize it as a replica of himself. "Would any man know himself clothed in such odd garments," he writes, "and set to caper and leer like a demon?"

The automaton turned from the path, and its fluidity of movement made Cornazzano momentarily believe the thing must be an actor in heavy makeup or mask, merely pretending to be a machine. But there were subtle inhumanities to its gestures that soon convinced him otherwise. Just as one could never mistake the mechanical chrysanthemum for a real flower, neither could one think this object was a man.

The creature fled across the garden, black boots flickering over the grass, and was it any wonder that Cornazzano left the safety of the path to chase his double, hungry for a better look? The automaton darted playfully beneath an evening sky as dark as iron. It ran through a swamp of reeds that hummed sad flute-song, and then across a plain of grass which rippled, though there was no breeze in the air.

Cornazzano watched as his replica slipped into one of the many grottoes that were too smooth for nature. No longer the agile danseur he'd once been, he found himself winded at the entrance to the cave and stopped, considering whether he should continue following the creature. His blond hair lay wet against his forehead. His gut heaved. He knew he should walk away—leave Francini to his madness. But still some part of him wanted to doubt what his eyes had recorded. It was not possible that Francini had built his own Cornazzano to live in his garden of gods.

Cornazzano writes, *I crept into the cave and found the creature no longer dancing but crouched near one wall, huddled in its tunic as if for warmth. Seeing the details of my own face—or rather the details of how I had once been, a young and foolish boy—gave rise to an intense and surprising anger. I wondered if Francini was making a mockery of me, or worse, if perhaps he used this metal man for some type of pleasure. And I found myself gripping the thing's pallid face, feeling the contours of its chin and cheeks. I pulled at its nose which was made of some soft metal, pushed at its eyes until the bulbs of glass cracked beneath my thumbs. The automaton did not struggle. It allowed its destruction. Perhaps that is even why it led me to the cave. And when I reached into the creature's mouth, trying to find some tongue to pull out, I heard behind me the scuff of a leather boot on the sandy cave floor.*

I turned to see Francini himself—hair shot with silver, eyes set deep in his skull, standing and watching in the fading light. This was not my laughing friend from Florence with bright eyes and wine-stained lips. This was a poor copy—an old man—ruined and sad.

"What have you done?" he asked in a soft voice.

By then I had managed to rip the automaton's lower jaw from its head, and I tossed it at Francini's feet. "That question," I said, "would be better put to you, maestro."

"I thought you would like him, 'Tonio," Francini whispered. He bent to pick up the jaw from the cave floor, and as

The Automatic Garden

I formulated some rebuke, feeling the old dangers and passions rushing back into the causeways of my heart, I realized something was wrong. Francini's fingers were around the jaw bone, but he did not grasp it, nor did he attempt to straighten himself. He had grown intensely still in his awkward, bent position, and it was only then that I realized—this was not Francini. It was not even alive.

Such horror I felt. I could not move my arms or legs, could not look at this false Francini with limp gray hair hanging against its brow. I wondered if my old friend even still existed. I wanted to cry out for him. I wanted Francini to reveal himself in flesh and blood, but I held my tongue. How I escaped the automatic garden, I do not know. It seems to me that the gods called to me as I ran—begged me not to leave at first and then mocked me for my foolishness. And even as I sit composing these lines at my own wooden table in my home where I can hear the sound of my good wife speaking to my children in the upper rooms, I wonder if am I still in that garden, lying on the cave floor, broken into my separate parts.

There Are No Bodies Such as This

Berne, Switzerland 1765

A SEASON OF ICE descends upon the winter chalet, cracking mortar and spreading bright veins across the window glass. Water freezes in the kitchen's basins. The cat is found stiff and white in the orchard. Herr Curtius, the physician, tries to keep his warmth. He employs Madame's mother as housekeeper and fire stoker, and Madame herself, though nothing more than the servant's daughter, is permitted to sit by the hearth. The doctor smokes a dark French tobacco in his silk chair and talks to her. Having no children of his own, he is surprised that such simple companionship can be a cure for the maladies of winter. He gives her a tour of his cold operating chamber, shows her his scientific wax models—polished heart, near-black liver, and a brain that can be separated into halves. She listens as he tells her of his practice, and when her interests seem to wane, he turns to stories that his own mother once told by firelight—stories of the saints. Madame asks to hear again about Bishop Fisher, a saint beheaded by mad King Henry of England for crimes against the crown. The bishop's head was hung from a long spike on London Bridge, but rather than rot and fall away as flesh should do, the head remained intact, growing more beautiful by the day.

"As if made of your very own medical wax," Madame interrupts, and Herr Curtius nods at her observation.

He has explained that wax, like the soul, does not perish.

On the spike, the bishop's cheeks turn rosy, and his eyes dampen with a youthful dew. The citizens of London say he looks finer than he ever did in life, and the head becomes a spectacle that draws crowds who clog the narrow artery of London Bridge, bringing offerings of wheat and fresh butchered lamb, hoping to curry favor with God. The weight of the throngs threaten to send the whole bridge, precarious on the best of days, crashing into the icy river, and finally, authorities are forced to take matters in hand, pulling the head down and hurling it into the Thames where it is finally washed away.

"And what befell it then?" Madame asks.

Herr Curtius clears his throat, checking to ensure that her mother, the maid, is not listening. This could be considered a tale of horror, after all, if it were not about the life of a saint. "The head was most likely eaten by whatever fish dare swim in the filthy English river," he tells her.

She pretends amusement, but later, in bed beside her mother, Madame dreams an altogether different fate. The head of the saint is carried along by the cold black current, water passing across the bishop's open mouth, flowing fast enough to cause a rippling song. What song the head sings, she does not know. An old one, to be sure, the sort that only water and the dead can remember.

There Are No Bodies Such as This

The singing head is carried out of London and deposited on the sandy banks of a small farm where it is found by a girl not unlike Madame herself—a child who loves beauty in all its forms. She takes the saint's head home in her carrying basket and installs it behind a rough hewn drapery in her father's hayloft. The drape can be raised and lowered depending on the quality of the guest. Not everyone knows how to appreciate a miracle, after all. Once again, the flesh of the bishop's head does not decompose, and when news of this spectacle spreads to the nearby villages, the head begins to draw a wonderful crowd. The girl charges for her miracle, and she cannot collect money fast enough. A line forms at the door of the barn, and she thinks perhaps her mother can stop cleaning. Her father can put down his tools and be happy in life again.

Madame cannot help but compare her life to this girl's. Her own poor father won't be resurrected even by the glory of the saints. He died two months before she was born in a battle of the Seven Years War against English troops. At night instead of praying to God, Madame prays to her father, picturing his body fixed in the still ether of the Empyrean, starlight pouring through the holes in his chest. She has no likenesses of him and must rely on the mundane descriptions her mother has given. "He was tall, Marie. Taller than most. With a man's strong jaw and a dark mole upon his cheek." Madame would like to ask her mother to describe her father's soul—was it hot or was it wet? Was there daylight in him or was he a man of the evening?

She asks Herr Curtius if he would consider making a medical model of her father out of wax. She and her mother could provide details and the doctor would do the sculpting. Herr Curtius, amused, tells her he will consider the idea, and though Madame's father never materializes, it is in this way that the museum is born.

THIS NEW & POISONOUS AIR

Paris, 1778

THERE IS STILLNESS on the Champs Élysées. A woman in an ostrich feather hat pauses mid-step, one black boot visible beneath her skirts. A man stoops to retrieve his handkerchief and his shadow becomes a placid pool that will go undisturbed for centuries. This is the first scene in the wax museum—a frozen *tableau de Paris*. Patrons linger at the velvet rope, trying to catch the scent of live flowers in the air. Herr Curtius no longer practices medicine, having instead taken Madame and her mother to France to open his wax museum on the fashionable Place de le Concorde. Parisians flock to see his figures frozen in moments of beauty and valor. Most beloved is the figure of the Comptesse du Barry—mistress of Louis XV. She is displayed among baskets of roses, a frozen voluptuary in bows and pale silk. The low neckline of her dress reveals the pinkness of her skin. "Impossible to believe that such supple-looking breasts are made of wax," says a friend of Herr Curtius on a visit to the museum, nearly poking the figure's chest with the tip of his cane.

"Oh, but it is wax," the doctor assures him. "The secret to making fine figures is knowing that the wax must appear more beautiful than the flesh it imitates. There are no bodies such as this in life."

Madame takes lessons from Herr Curtius and proves a quick study. She molds accurate components of unreal bodies: the slender arm of a sleeping princess, a Roman soldier's foot, the emaciated torso of Christ. For her first full model, she will not attempt a lowly figure like the Comptesse du Barry, though she is humbled, of course, by Herr Curtius's knack for verisimilitude. "A figure of wax should be worthy," she tells the doctor. "Perhaps we are not making great art, but we must at least make great men." She chooses Jean-Jacques Rousseau, the philosopher. Unlike the Comtesse, Rousseau is no longer living, and Madame finds pleasure in his resurrection. She attempts to put the Enlightenment in the shape of Rousseau's face and paints his glass eyes a most delicate and knowing shade of gray. Herr Curtius proudly places Rousseau on a pedestal near the front of the museum, tucking a yellowed copy of *Confessions* in the model's pocket to make sure there is no question of identity. It is, after all, Madame's first attempt.

At Christmastime, the doctor presents her with a pair of wire-rimmed eyeglasses, saying he's noticed her squinting while sculpting her models. When she sets the frames on the bridge of her nose, it's as if a painted scrim has unfurled from invisible rafters in the museum's ceiling. Figures that she's made with her own hands—Rabelais and Sir Philip the Good—are new to her, standing cleanly before the plum-colored drapes. Sunlight falls in sharp lines across the eyes of Denis Diderot as if he wears a bright mask. Gray moths flutter in the lace ruff around the neck of Anne of Cleaves. When Madame turns to thank Herr Curtius for his marvelous gift, she finds that he is gone, and she hurries down the corridor where patrons queue during business hours to find the doctor smoking in the antechamber, oaken door opened onto the boulevard and a pile of snow forming on the carpet at his feet.

"I am embarrassed that I have nothing for you, doctor," she says.

He does not respond, lost in some thought. Finally, when she touches his sleeve, he turns. "There is nothing that I need, Marie, other than your presence."

She cannot meet his glance. Gently, he lays his hand against her cheek.

When nothing is left of the holiday season but gray ice and a few forgotten ornaments, Herr Curtius tells Madame over a supper of cold lamb that the cost of the museum's operation has proved greater than his estimation. "We may need to move our establishment," he says, "find an area of cheaper rent. I'm sure you've noticed the crowds here are dwindling."

"Do you think it's due to my poor modeling?" she asks. "My eyeglasses have improved the accuracy of my work greatly."

He takes a careful bite of lamb. "It is possible that Paris has simply had enough of wax. I could always practice medicine again. You will live comfortably, Marie, I promise you."

"I don't want to live comfortably, Herr Curtius," she replies. "I want to live as mistress of a wax museum with you as its master."

Madame redoubles her efforts of creation, and during this trial, she nearly forgets her mother who, out of boredom, dusts the wax figures each evening, running delicate feathers over the wig of Benjamin Franklin, the boots of Voltaire, and the makeshift helmet of Don Quixote. When her mother, thick and eager, urges her once again to begin searching for a husband, Madame replies that she has Herr Curtius, who is neither father nor husband but something more, and on top of that, she has her wax. "Wax will not make you children, Marie," her mother says, tears growing in her eyes. Madame points toward the gallery where the figures loom. Her fingers ache and there is wax beneath her nails as well as burn scars on her palms. "If not children, Mother," she says sharply, "what are these?"

One evening, there is a desperate knocking at Madame's bedroom door, and she opens it to find Herr Curtius in his nightdress, cheeks white, hair dense with sweat. He looks older than Madame ever imagined him to be, and he tells her of a terrible nightmare, all the more awful because it seemed real. He dreamed there was a secret door behind a curtain in the wax museum, a door made of rough cheap wood, like a poor man's coffin, and it opened onto a cave filled with figures the likes of which no modern man has ever seen. He clutches her arm. "Marie," he whispers, "I must be going mad to have dreamed such things—piercing instruments of medieval torture, a black pharaoh with a stone scarab on his tongue, Judas leering with his silver coins, and Brutus—hands gloved in Caesar's blood—howling from his pedestal. Why would God send such a dream, Marie? You must tell me. I'll trust your answer."

She blushes at his confidence and considers the dream of the hidden chamber. Perhaps it is some allegory. Or a foretelling of the future by way of symbols from the past. But then she realizes it may be a simple directive. "A chamber like the one you describe would draw a fine crowd, I think," she says.

Herr Curtius sits heavily on the edge of her bed, staring at his hands. "People will pay to see horrors from a dream?"

"That will be the art of it, Doctor Curtius," Madame replies. "Our visitors will *enter* your dream—a dark sister to our beautiful museum—and when they leave that chamber, they will feel as though they are waking, and gladly so. You must write down all that you remember. We will begin work immediately."

"You told me our figures must be noble," he says.

She kisses him lightly on the cheek. "It was God who sent the dream, not me."

Later she discovers a detail about the chamber that the doctor could not bring himself to tell. It is scribbled in the margins of his papers. At the back of the chamber of horrors, he found himself lying flat on a wooden board, the kind they used when beginning to carve a model. His skin glowed with a waxy sheen—like a dead man in funeral makeup. And it was not at all clear whether the body was made of wax or of flesh. This frightened him more than all of history's horrors combined.

Paris, 1781

THE CHAMBER OF HORRORS is not completed before Herr Curtius, beautiful and kind, succumbs to a disease of the liver. Madame is overwhelmed by the loss and spends much of her time with the vile bodies in the darkened room. She installs a magic lantern machine and using candlelight and a series of lenses, she is able to create the illusion of movement. Hell-flames spark and lick the boots of patrons. Shadows detach from figures and slip across the walls, shrinking and expanding like lungs. The ghost of Herr Curtius himself—a trick of filtered light—is seen passing through the chamber, surveying his attraction.

She is still in mourning when she marries the young engineer, François Tussaud. It is a marriage of necessity. The doctor left her his wax museum, and she needs a husband to help with the work. A woman cannot sculpt alone nor steer an enterprise so lucrative. There is also the revolution building among the urban poor—a slow-heating oven of resentment stoked by the ridiculous lawyer, Robespierre, with his misshapen head, whom Madame refuses to make in wax, though he has written her a personal note of request. She has heard rumors of his plans for uprising—a so-called Reign of Terror—and she needs protection. But she wishes that her wedding dress could have been painted black to wipe the satisfaction from her mother's face.

Tussaud is, at first, the walled city she hoped him to be. The unbroken line of his mustache, his starched collars and pressed pants—he seems a strong breed of architecture. But not a year into their marriage, he reveals himself to be unscrupulous with money, spending so extravagantly that Madame worries he may cause finances for the museum to fail.

When she lies next to him at night, she stills her heart and stops her thoughts, attempting to exist as the simulacrum of Marie Tussaud, more eloquent and obedient a wife than the real woman could ever be. But even in this petrifaction, she is aware of the pendulum inside her, swinging first back to childhood where she sits at the feet of the doctor wondering what the future will bring, and then into the future where she stands in a beautiful room that is empty of her sculptures. The room itself—molding, sconces, marble floor—is a sculpture, all made of wax, and when she opens the door there is another city, greater than Paris, all of it glittering with the workmanship of her own hand. Beyond the city, there are waxen meadows and a painted sky. It appears as though she has made a country for herself, if not a universe. She is not meant for Tussaud. She will not let him ruin her.

She admits she is pleased when the new placard is raised, "Madame Tussaud's House of Wax." She stands in the crowd with François at her side. He leans close enough to touch her ear with the fringe of his mustache and whispers, "What part of the museum would the famous Madame Tussaud like to survey on her inaugural visit?"

"The Chamber of Horrors, I think," she says softly.

"Really, my dear? All that grim fantasy and blood?"

"There is no fantasy about it, François. It is an embryo, a showing of what is to come."

Paris, 1789

MADAME IS EVERYWHERE renowned. The king himself loves her figures of wax, and he brings her to Versailles where she is to make models of the royal court. He wants to display these figures in the grand ballroom so courtiers can dance among their replicas. "They can even ask *themselves* to dance if they so choose," he says. Madame realizes the king has made a joke, but she cannot smile. The little man reminds her of Tussaud. He is foolish with money and finds himself all too important. He sees no real gravity in wax. When she molds his figure, she presses her thumb into his chest, making a hole above the place where his heart would be.

Madame meets Marie Antoinette in the garden's palisades among the lime trees. The two have not yet been introduced and because the young queen is costumed in strange rural clothes with her fair hair curled naturally at the side of her neck, Madame does not recognize her. The queen, Madame expects, would be a bright wedding cake of a woman, complete with towering coiffure built of pads and powder. But on this particular day, Marie Antoinette has been at Petit Trianon, the mock farmhouse on the palace grounds where she goes with her friends to tend sheep, and in peasant's garb, she is like any other girl of seventeen, beautiful in the sunlight. She asks if she might try on Madame's wire-framed eyeglasses, and Madame hands them over, saying, "They were a gift from someone I loved."

The girl places the eyeglasses on the bridge of her nose and stands staring up into the lime trees. Madame watches, thinking how she would never make such a creature in wax. There is nothing about the girl that would draw an audience, and yet it is pleasant to see her living and walking in the garden. Some people are simply not meant to be memorialized—such effigy would detract from their beauty and life.

"Do you see the fruit more clearly now, my dear?" Madame asks.

"Oh, no. These glasses make me blind," says the girl. Then she turns her attention on Madame, eyes looming from behind the lenses. "Are you the wax woman from Paris?"

"I am Madame Tussaud. That is correct."

The girl nods. "I should like to take a lesson or two. Do you give lessons?"

"Not as a rule," Madame replies.

The girl seems saddened. "I would have liked to learn to make dolls for my children. They're babies, you know, and all their dolls seem terribly formal."

"Well, wax is not a toy either," Madame replies.

The girl removes the eyeglasses, hands them delicately to Madame, and wanders off into the lime trees without another word. It is only later that Madame realizes her error, though Marie Antoinette pretends not to remember their conversation in the palisades, as if, for a few moments, she was in fact a peasant girl with no relationship to the crown.

Paris, 1793

FRANÇOIS TUSSAUD IS AWAY when the Reign of Terror erupts, spreading fire and revolution through the city. Madame is dragged from her museum by a band of common men in shepherds' pants and muddied blouses. The boulevard is filled with smoke, and a man screams for mercy in the distance. When Madame begs them to explain what crime she has committed, their leader says she is under suspicion for Royalist sympathies. "You have been to Versailles, done work for the king." She thinks of the hole she put above King Louis' heart, and she wants to explain, but how can a thing like that be put into words?

Madame is imprisoned. Her head is shaved, and they carry her hair away in a wicker basket. They take her eyeglasses despite her pleading, and she stifles tears the entire night, thinking of Herr Curtius, glad that he is not alive to suffer such cruelties. It is in prison that she meets Josephine de Beauharnais, who will one day become the wife of Emperor Napoleon. Madame's hands ache when she sees Lady Josephine. She wishes to preserve her in wax—to make this idol permanent before she disappears. Finally, after weeks of waiting, Madame is set free under the condition that she will use her skills to make death masks of the royal family. She does not protest. She does as she is ordered. When she is taken to the room where Marie Antoinette's head is waiting, she finds she cannot approach the table. Beneath a rough cloth there is a shape the size of a serving pitcher. A crescent of brown blood has seeped through the material. And when a jar of wax is placed in her hands—beeswax, her medium of choice— Madame can hear the sound of the bees that made it. The wax itself is frightened. It does not want to approach the head of the queen.

The guard—or the fool in rags who calls himself a guard—moves toward the table.

"Wait a moment," Madame says, though she does not know what duration would be required to prepare herself for what she is about to see. She thinks there is a hint of smile on the guard's face as he removes the cloth, and she is confronted with the object—which cannot rightly be called a head because it no longer sits upon shoulders of the queen. Marie Antoinette's face is not well preserved. She was not a saint like Bishop Fisher on London Bridge. There is only fear and surprise in the girl's clouded eyes. It appears as if something has eaten away a portion of her lower lip.

When Madame is allowed to return to her museum, which was only partially destroyed by fire, she will make a secret figure in wax that will never be displayed, a copy of herself as she looked in prison, head shaved and without eyeglasses. She deepens the eyeholes until they are caverns, elongates the jaw into a wolflike muzzle. And when she is finished with the monster—while the wax is still warm—she pounds her fist against the thing, weeping and wishing more than anything else that she had taught the queen to make the foolish dolls for her children.

London, 1802

WHEN MADAME ARRIVES in London, both she and her figures are broken. The models have not travelled well, despite the packing straw. Severed hands, pieces of leg and, unbearably, a head or two are lifted carefully from their crates by her new staff and placed in the laboratory for reattachment. But she does not know if she can put all of history back together again. The line of sense is broken.

"Tussauds House of Wax" will open in the Baker Street Bazaar between the Punch's Theater and the House of Mystery—as if Herr Curtius's grand museum is some carnival joke. Madame has removed the apostrophe from her surname on the placard. She no longer wants to claim the wax museum, and she does not speak of her past nor of the husband and aged mother she left in France. She will never go back to that country again, never see Paris. Not after what they have done. The head of Marie Antoinette, of Louis XVI, and finally even of Robespierre himself haunts her hands. She cannot forget. Her husband will write letters, imploring her to return, but he will never come looking. Perhaps he is afraid he could no longer distinguish Madame Tussaud from her figures. He will be halfway home before he realizes he has pulled the wrong woman from the wax museum. What he took for his wife will be melting in the sun.

She does not often visit the garish museum. Instead, she takes walks in the city. Imagine a woman dressed in gathered French silk, standing on the planks of London Bridge. Her graying hair is pinned carefully beneath her fashionable hat; a new pair of eyeglasses rests upon her nose. She studies the tall wooden houses that recede in every direction beneath a pall of black soot in the sky. She has made few acquaintances in this city. Unlike Paris, London is a business arrangement. Looking down into the rushing current of the Thames, she rests one hand on the bridge railing while the other hangs limply at her side. Water, she thinks, is nothing like wax. It is impermanent. It does not glorify. She wishes she could have carved her famous figures out of water, so they immediately fell from their pedestals, splashing into puddles on the floor. Such a display might have provided a more accurate depiction. For if there are saints, Madame knows they are few, and none of them are remembered for long.

Fall, Orpheum

DAVID MILLER AND HIS SISTER, Kitty, almost didn't go to the theater on the night she disappeared. After getting into a fight with a boy at school, Kitty lay on the leather sofa at the Miller house, staring at the shadows of moths caught in the beveled globe of the ceiling fan, whispering oaths about how she'd never again make another mistake with her heart. David sat rocking in the corner chair, still dressed in his grassy baseball jersey and wearing cleats in the house despite his mother's wishes. He felt restless from an evening of pitching drills and tried reasoning with his sister, saying the movie wasn't a love story—it was about men looking for a diamond in the jungles of Peru. Cheeks flushed and a pillow clutched to her chest, Kitty said that looking for diamonds in the jungle was just like looking for love, and if the stupid king of baseball was too dense to understand metaphor, she didn't want to go anywhere with him anyway. He grabbed her legs and pulled her roughly off the sofa, wrestling her to the floor. This was enough to finally rouse her, and as she adjusted her tank top, she said, "All right, David. Let's go see if they find that stupid rock."

He was relieved, though he'd never show Kitty how much. He knew he was, in fact, the stupid king of baseball and saw the world as a series of outlines. Kitty knew how to fill in the blanks. To him, she was like one of the statues at St. John's, long-limbed and tormented—a series of miraculous meditations.

We understood David's love. On Tuesday nights at women's basketball games, we rooted for Kitty Miller, admiring the sharp curve of her ponytail and the way her eyes caught light from the blond gymnasium floor. At seventeen, she was still an arrow of time, pointing us toward our own graceful moments of youth. She took care of our children, served plates of egg casserole at church brunches, and helped the Founder's Daughters fold paper flowers to decorate empty shop windows. Despite all of this, we knew she was biding her time. Girls like Kitty weren't meant to grow old among our factory corridors and sawdust diners. Eventually, when she found a way, she'd leave. We'd seen it happen to other promising sons and daughters, though we thought, like them, she'd end up in some city, calling home twice a month to assure her mother and her brother that she was fine.

What we never imagined was that Kitty would be taken. How could such a thing happen to our girl? But Kitty rose halfway through the movie when the adventurers had assembled the collected pieces of a parchment map and found the entrance to the cave where the diamond was hidden. Wind blew across the cave mouth, and one of the adventurers, gaunt with exhaustion, said the noise sounded very much like regret. We wanted to stop Kitty, to pull her back. If nothing else, we wanted to save her for David's sake. But farmers and factory workers, teachers and clerks, we were each trapped in our roles.

The Orpheum Theater was our landmark after all, a sweet flycatcher in an otherwise unlovely town. How did the building become more than mere mortar and brick? If we had to guess, we'd say its transcendence was a product of our desiring. Everything that is desired is, in a sense, made flesh. We snuck off for afternoon matinees when we should have been building toolboxes at the plant and stayed late for midnight shows rather than making conversation under the dinner-plate moon at the reservoir. Our mothers hadn't been able to warn us about work not doing itself because they too had spent their time in the Orpheum's thrall, sometimes barely remembering to feed us. When visitors came, they were drawn to our theater, if not to sit for a movie, then just to marvel at the abundance of its Oriental bric-a-brac: silk-tasseled mirrors, brass elephant heads, brèche violette pillars, and foreign deities that peered from every corner of the stonework. The auditorium was a walled courtyard, complete with an accurately constellated sky and a procession of clouds projected on the black ceiling by a magic lantern machine, and the pale glow that fell on us night after night was like a hunter's jack-light, pulling animals helplessly from the brush.

David thought his sister needed to use the theater's restroom, but when she simply remained standing at her seat, blocking the view of those behind her, he touched her hand and whispered, "Kit, you feeling okay?" Her gaze drifted from the tense scene at the jungle cave to the black door beneath the movie screen, the one we told ourselves was the entrance to a storage room or simply an unmarked exit. We said these things to avoid saying the door was a way of climbing inside the Orpheum's skin. "We can leave if you want," David said. "Maybe this wasn't such a hot idea." Without responding, Kitty began to walk down the center aisle, a bride in khaki shorts and a tank top that revealed arms and legs as smooth as stone. Of course, David stood to follow her, and we don't know which of us dropped the white candy at his feet. All those brittle pieces, like so many broken teeth. It was awful to watch such a sure young sportsman fall. By the time David had righted himself, his sister had already opened the black door beneath the screen and stepped inside, closing it softly behind. David tried the knob. "Kitty," he whispered, "Come on, Kit. This isn't funny." When she didn't respond, he turned to look at us, searching our faces for the possibility of help. On the screen, a man with a sweat-beaded brow held the diamond as big as his fist, unaware that he was about to be struck by a poison dart.

In the weeks before her disappearance, the Orpheum had started to become for Kitty what it was for all of us—a kind of gentle mystery, easing us along, never providing enough clues to disturb us from our sleep. She was seventeen after all, old enough to begin her awakening, and David was a sturdy vessel for her confidences. "The air inside that place goes all the way through me, but it doesn't feel cold," she told him, as they sat on the bench at Ray's Creamery, both eating piles of vanilla ice cream with plastic spoons. The Orpheum loomed across the street, an arabesque palace, the evening sun turning its gold leaf a livid shade of red.

David swatted a fly away from his sunburned leg. "It's called air-conditioning, Kit. What they won't think of next, right?"

"Have you been listening to me at all?"

"Sure," he said.

"Then don't make stupid comments, David. I'm talking about atmosphere. That place has started to make me feel like it's filling me with air from another planet. Like I'm a balloon, full of some other world. Maybe you have to be older to understand."

"A balloon, really? That's one of the dumbest things I've ever heard you say. Maybe you just have to turn your brain back on and realize it's just a plain old movie theater."

"It's not," Kitty replied. "At least not to me anymore."

He turned his dusty baseball cap backward, considering the shade of his sister's eyes that balanced somewhere between blue and green. "Okay, balloon-girl" he said. "I give up. What is it?"

Across the street, the gaudy plastic vines wound around the theater's marble pillars. "I'm not sure," she said, "but I think all the movies they've shown there over the years have given it ideas."

David gave her a half-smile. "So what kind of ideas does a movie theater have?"

"It thinks that it could do better," Kitty said quietly. "All those stories are so ordinary. It wants to show us something truly marvelous."

"Come on," he said, though his tone betrayed unease. The Orpheum was better off left to silence. "I think town council should tear that shack down and give us stadium seats and cup holders."

"I'd chain myself to the doors," Kitty said. "People who do stupid things like that don't understand history."

He squinted at a particularly malicious-looking stone monkey that peered from one corner of the Orpheum's jade roof. "The nut that sells the tickets—old white braids—would beat you to it," he said. "She'd shoot Mike and Ike's out of

37

every hole in her body to fend off the bulldozers."

"Don't be disgusting, David," Kitty said. "May Avalon is just—lonely."

"Have you heard some of that weird music she plays on her record player?" he asked. "I mean, who even *has* a record player anymore?"

She scraped her spoon against the bottom of her ice cream bowl. "The thing about old music is that none of it sounds the way it's supposed to anymore because we just don't have the right ears to hear it."

After pretending to consider this, David licked his finger and stuck it deep in Kitty's ear. She screamed and leapt from the bench. "There you go, Kit," he said. "Now, go float away."

Poor Kitty went to the bathroom to wash, and we kept our distance from the scene. If David Miller was right about anything, it was that the ticket seller, May Avalon, would chain herself to the theater to save it. In a sense, she already had, manning her glass booth for nearly sixty years, a wooden woman on the prow of a sunken ship, submerged but unable to drown. With her white hair still in girlish braids, she pushed the button to dispense pink tickets without giving our faces so much as a single glance. Old songs drifted from her antique record player, music from the vaudeville age that conjured images of singing puppets, garish blackface and fluttering Chinese silk. We knew her history well enough—had heard it repeated by our parents and grandparents. If the theater was a body, May Avalon was not its heart but its liver, performing a hundred mysterious functions, and her despair was nearly as much a landmark as the Orpheum itself.

May had lost her only love to the theater years ago—a towheaded buck dancer named Common Woolbrink who traveled the vaudeville circuit, performing on the flame-lit stages of small towns across the Midwest. Unlike his shabby costume, Woolbrink's dancing was said to be a modern marvel. His colorless eyes recognized the world anew every time he looked out over an audience, and he danced with such vigor that he required an oak platform on which to perform for fear that he might break through the pinewood stage. If women watched him too long, they fainted. Men were driven to riot.

What burned him into our town's collective memory was not his dancing but his death—stabbed eleven times with a hunting knife on the steps of the Orpheum by a man named Roy Elkhart who said Woolbrink had lied at a game of cards. May Avalon, then just a girl, held the boy's head in her lap and ran her fingers through his hair like she was his mother, watching blood pool on the concrete. She undid the clasps of his red dancing shoes, and after they took his body away, sat holding them to her chest, not five feet from where she'd spend the rest of her life selling tickets. The Orpheum transitioned from vaudeville house to movie palace, and May remained. "Picture shows are safer than live acts," one man was quoted as saying in *The Monitor*. "They can't be pig-stuck—no matter how much we hate the act."

If Common Woolbrink's death was the Orpheum's first real tragedy, then Kitty Miller's disappearance was to be its last. One week after she and her brother sat eating ice cream at Ray's, she was gone, and David Miller, T-shirt torn and blood on his cheek, pulled the first piece of concrete from the crumbling steps, aiming it at the Orpheum. He threw his stone, not at the glass ticket booth, nor at the grand marquee that sprouted birds' nests like untrimmed hair. Instead, he aimed at one of the Egyptian crocodile gods that flanked the theater's entrance, using the smooth motion he'd learned from a summer of practices, believing that at least those toothy, moon-eyed gods provided a face for the Orpheum's mysteries. But we knew the sculptures were little more than monster masks, products of the 1923 renovation. If anyone was to blame for Kitty's disappearance, it was not the gods but us—we who'd been losing control of our house of dreams for years.

David was too young to know about the others, but what happened to Kitty had happened before. There'd been the black girl who'd come on the bus, no more than thirteen, carrying a backpack full of clothes with a doll tied to it. She looked like the kind of child who'd been hollowed out by life. When she went to the Orpheum, we assumed she intended to wash herself in its bathroom sink and then lose her worries in a movie for a while. May Avalon even gave her a free pass, something the old crone was loath to do for any of us. The girl left her backpack in a pool of soda, and we put the dirty thing in the garbage when the lights came on.

There'd also been the young man who slicked his hair and tucked his shirts and affected melancholy even when working at the toolbox factory. We knew his sort. When he talked about the movies, he said he still dreamed of being part of them, an idea that was tedious, and when he disappeared behind the black door, we told ourselves he'd run away to live some other life. Having a family and watching movies weren't good enough for him.

And finally, there'd been Lon Stellmacher, the Stellmachers' retarded son who was such a burden to his parents, he made Beth look old before her time and forced Carl to put away all his hearty ambitions. Poor Lon almost didn't make it down the aisle because he had trouble seeing in the dark. When he stumbled against a row of seats, a few of us reached out and put him back on his way. Beth and

Carl blamed themselves for letting him go to the Orpheum alone, but we didn't place such blame. Even watchfulness and care have their limits.

David Miller didn't know that we'd been observing disappearances for years, never quite thinking of them as sacrifices. We knew only that our parents had done the same as us, and their parents before that. Any one of our grandparents could have stopped Roy Elkhart before he stabbed Common Woolbrink eleven times, but instead they stood by and marveled at the way his wounds opened like mouths in his red coat.

David didn't call for our help on the night Kitty slipped behind the black door. Instead, he merely stared at us there in our threadbare seats, still dressed in our work clothes, the expression on his face becoming a kind of mirror. On the day-bright streets, he knew most of us by name, but in the Orpheum, we were different, a single organism, immense yet paralyzed, and our beautiful theater, with all its rich trappings and pictures of youth, was nothing more than a funeral hall, holding services, night after night, for the same powdered corpse. Perhaps what frightened David the most was not our empty faces but the fact that so many seats in the Orpheum remained empty too, like invitations to sit for a show.

In the lobby, May Avalon reclined, eyes buried in blue makeup, listening to the cheerful voices drifting from her record player. Her pale fingers played absently against the seam of her nylon pants.

"Something happened to my sister," David said breathlessly, having run the length of the aisle and burst into the lobby.

With effort, May roused herself, white braids brushing the shoulders of her uniform blouse. "What did you say?"

"Kitty, my sister," he said. "She got up and walked away."

May attempted a smile. "Kitty's quite an old-fashioned named isn't it? Maybe the movie didn't agree with her. These sorts are for men. We have a woman's story coming next week."

He took off his baseball cap and folded the brim, trying in earnest to stay calm. "She didn't leave, ma'am. She went through that door under the screen and now she's locked in."

Her smile became a colorless line. "Are you sure?"

"Of course I am," he said.

"It usually only happens if they're alone," she said.

"Happens?"

May lifted a pair of gold-rimmed glasses from the ticket console and put them carefully on her nose, studying David's damp blond hair. "Do I know you?" she said.

He shrugged. "You've been selling me tickets all my life. Me and Kitty."

Taking off her glasses, she sighed. "That makes you no different than the rest of them, I suppose. But I can see you care about your sister. She must be a darling."

"The rest of who, lady? What are you talking about?"

"My name is May, dear," she said. "It's better if you call me by my name."

He took a deep breath. "Look, May, my sister is locked behind the door under the screen. She *is* a . . . darling, I guess. But she's sad tonight because of a stupid thing that happened with some guy. Something that shouldn't bother her because so many people at school are just in love with her. I just need you to unlock the door so I can get her out and take her home. Please. May."

The old woman lifted the needle from the turning record, bringing silence to the lobby. "I can try," she said, pulling a blue sweater from the back of her chair. "For you, because you remind me of someone I knew once. Another darling."

David didn't bother to ask what she meant and instead simply followed her into the cold auditorium, down the darkened aisle to the door. She put a key from the ring around her wrist into the lock and whispered, "The manager doesn't like anyone going up here. We've had some problems." The smell that wafted from the space beyond was intensely sweet, unlike anything David had ever experienced—perfume from another place. And as they ascended the wooden staircase behind the door, he whispered, "Is this where you keep all the movie candy or something?"

"No, dear," May said. "We keep that in the basement. This area isn't for storage."

They arrived at a long empty room made of pinewood planks, and it took David a moment to realize that he was looking at a portion of the old vaudeville stage that his grandfather had told him about, complete with rusted footlights and a hinged trapdoor. Abandoned flats leaned against one wall—trees cut from plywood, the circle of a lover's moon hung from a wire, and finally there was a wooden city, hastily painted yet still evocative—perhaps all part of some long-forgotten act. The city drew David's attention. Walled and turreted like a medieval fortress, its streets and bridges made little sense, wandering until they eventually disappeared. People could get lost on streets like those, especially if they didn't know their way. The city was empty—no painted version of Kitty there. He pulled his attention away from it and pointed at the trapdoor that was wide enough to raise a small piano. "Could she have fallen down there?" he asked.

"Was your sister the clumsy sort?" May asked, as she unwound a tattered rope from a hook and allowed the trapdoor to drop, revealing a dark pit, from which rose another potent blast of candied air. David knelt beside the hole and called his sister's name, and when no one answered, he said, "We have to get some light. Maybe she can't talk because she's hurt."

"She's not," May said.

He looked at her sharply.

"She isn't down there, dear, and she isn't coming back," she continued. "I should have told you that before, but part of me just wanted to see you on this stage. They never come back. God knows I've looked for my own in here."

"Your own?"

"Common," she said, reaching out her long arms to David. In the light that seeped through the spaces between the wooden planks, May could have been any age—maybe a girl, looking into another boy's eyes, years ago.

Our town doctor had once requested that Common Woolbrink sit for an examination so that he might learn the secrets of the boy's agility. It was at this examination that May Avalon met the handsome young buck dancer, as she was acting as an assistant to the nurse, her braids then as dark as her eyes, and the red stripes of her uniform so bright they could have been woven from flame. She was an intelligent girl and knew when to smile. May and Common chatted while he sat on the doctor's table, and afterward he invited her to the drugstore for a soda. At the chrome counter of the soda fountain, he told her the real secret to moving so fast—the one he'd never tell any doctor—he drank a daily dose of vegetable juice infused with a cutting from a mysterious and nameless root, provided to him by a Chinaman in St. Louis. When May pressed him to show her the root, he finally relented, producing a piece of it, which he kept in his pocket as a kind of talisman. The sight of Common Woolbrink holding the shriveled, rust-colored knob with so much reverence was enough to make May choke on her soda. She put the glass carefully on the counter, folded her hands and said that his magic root was nothing but a regular piece of ginger, and she could make him a cake of it for Christmas if he liked and then he could dance even faster.

We don't know the boy's response because the soda jerk who'd recorded the conversation until that point moved away so as not to appear to be spying, but if Woolbrink acted in character, he probably made up a lie to cover his embarrassment. Roy Elkhart knew Common was a liar, just as our grandparents did. A boy so bombastic couldn't always tell the truth. It soon became clear that May liked to hear Common's lies almost as much as he liked to tell them. According to him, he'd traveled halfway around the world, performing in English taverns, German cabarets, and even the floating show houses of Venice. May knew that a boy too poor to buy a suit that fit hadn't really traveled the world, but she stopped calling Common's bluffs and simply learned to revel in the details of his imagination. We know little of their relationship's progression, only that they were seen together when Common was in town and that May eventually wore his ring, a boyish bit of junk shop glamour in the form of an oversized diamond made of sugar that glittered madly in the sun.

In matters of love, the element least understood by outsiders often provides the glue, and there was, in fact, a final mystery to their story, a detail we could only see dimly. Common Woolbrink once whispered a secret so awful in May's ear that she didn't speak to him for nearly three weeks, only returning after a succession of bouquets and promises that he would never tell such a lie again. Apparently he'd gone too far with one of his confabulations, confessing to have traveled beyond the fair stages of Europe. Dancing, he said, was good for more than mere entertainment, and if the right dancer moved backward in a certain way, he could open doors to another place where everything was backward. Smoke was sucked into chimneys. Men returned home before leaving for work. And food was spat onto plates. Everyone there got younger instead of older. When May herself talked to him there, for she existed in that world just as everyone had a double, her teeth were actually on the outside of her mouth. Kissing her, he said, was like kissing a bed of stones.

May began to watch Common for any sign that his habitual lying was an expression of some mental infirmity, but he never spoke of the backward place or anything like it again. He was courteous and jovial. The lies he told were sweet, not frightening, and when he kissed her, he acted as though he had no memory of their stony kisses in that other world. It was only as he lay on the steps of the Orpheum, red coat darkened with redder blood, that he spoke of it again. Our grandparents crowded around the pair, and the sky must have looked to Common like a dome supported by their curious faces, with May's own hung closest, a beautiful child in mourning. At a safe distance, some of the stronger men held Roy Elkhart on the ground, and he howled for his hunting knife to be returned. People had to lean in close to hear Common say, "I left them open, May. Every single door is standing wide in there."

"Don't make things up," she whispered. "There's not

time for that."

He grimaced, one hand fluttering to touch her wrist. "If I don't shut them, no one will. People are going to fall."

May forced herself not to scream. This wasn't the ending she'd pictured. This wasn't the way to end. When she looked at blond David Miller on that dimly lit stage, some sixty years after Common was buried, she couldn't muster such control. She understood the clock-springs of love were more fragile than a young girl could have ever known. "You're younger by a few years," she whispered to David Miller, "but that's what happens there isn't it? You told me so. People age backward. I didn't believe you. I thought you were lying. But you're him."

David started to say he didn't know what she was talking about, but it was already too late. May was pulling him close. "We'll go through the door ourselves," she said. "I can be young again too, away from this place. I won't mind about your teeth. I promise I won't." And then she drew close to him, searching for some reassurance that he was who she wanted him to be—her beautiful liar without his red suit.

David Miller ran down the wooden staircase and burst through the black door. He would call his parents, and they would call the police, and all of them would call for Kitty until they'd lost their breath. They would question May, trying to understand the things she'd said that night, but the old woman would give them no straight answers, feigning confusion and turning up the volume on her record player. And as the days went by without any sign of Kitty, David Miller would come to believe that if he wanted his sister back, he'd have to take matters in hand.

When he finally pulled a piece of loose concrete from the steps outside the Orpheum and threw it at one of the upright crocodiles that flanked the entrance, only a few of us were there to see. He threw a second stone that shattered the glass poster case, and more of us came spilling from stores and houses to watch the boy. A few of us tried to stop him at first but only halfheartedly, knowing what had to be done. We no longer wanted to be the sort of thing that could not act. The kind of body that deserves a funeral every night.

It took our strongest backs to do the initial work, breaking down the Orpheum's glass doors, ripping the ornaments from the marquee, but by the end, even the weakest among us were able to get some of the work done, smashing the windows of the ticket booth and causing pink tickets to spiral onto the ground, destroying the concession stand, scattering popcorn and bright candy. We broke the decorative mirrors, pulled down the plastic vines, and threw May Avalon's record player against the pipe organ. But it was David Miller, T-shirt streaked and chest heaving, who actually found the old ticket seller, cowering on her knees in a row of empty seats. He pulled May to her feet and looked into her frightened face, covered with the same gray dust that churned in the air. "Now you tell me," he said, voice breaking. "You tell me, you old witch, without any of your crazy talk, where my sister is. You know, don't you? You've known all along."

Before she could answer, one of us struck her in the shoulder with a metal pipe, and as she was falling, another drove a piece of molding against her temple. If we were giving a confession, perhaps we would say we did this to test the flesh of the Orpheum against the flesh of the woman. Or maybe we would tell the truth, that we'd always hated May Avalon for knowing things we didn't. David watched her fall, then stood over her sprawled and unmoving body. He seemed to hesitate as she groped feebly with one hand to touch his shoe, not a dancing shoe at all, and finally with all his strength, David Miller kicked the old woman in the stomach. She didn't make a sound, and we had to look away from the terrible expression on her face.

Our razing of the Orpheum made the news as far away as Chicago, and when they saw pictures of what we'd done, they thought the whole town had lost its mind. Mob rule, they called it. Psychologists were interviewed and said our actions could very well be the product of the modern nihilism fed by the movies themselves. No outsider could understand our motivations though, nor could they know that after we'd finished our job, when many of us had been hauled off to bleach-smelling cots in the nearby jail, we shared a dream.

In the dream, we saw Kitty Miller injured and dragging her body, hand over fist, down a country road outside of town. A flat moon hung in the sky, nothing but a stage prop, and the trees at the sides of the road were the sketches of an untrained artist. Kitty was no longer just a girl. Her pretty cheeks were made of brick and mortar, her eyes as white as screens. Even her once lush hair looked more like the old birds' nests that sprouted from beneath the Orpheum's marquee.

In the distance stood a walled city, hastily painted, and on the shining streets of that city were the missing— Lon Stellmacher and the girl who came on the bus and the young man who wanted to be in the movies. There were so many more whom we didn't know, those who'd come before our time. And at the very head of the crowd was a blond boy dressed in a top hat and red tuxedo jacket, too tight around the shoulders. His face was a lamp, his eyebrows arched and white. He watched our girl approach and seemed to appraise us. We, who could no longer dress ourselves in the chilly air of our Orpheum, who could only watch as he gathered Kitty Miller in his arms. Common

Woolbrink gave us a final warning glance before turning on his heel and pulling shut the tall wooden gate of the city, leaving us to darkness. Knowing that this, after all, was what we'd wanted.

A Memory of His Rising

December 17, 19—

YOUNG MEN MOST COMMONLY REPORT *dreams of flight*—this passage taken from my father's professional journal. *A recent patient was subject to such realistic floating that, upon waking, he leapt from his bed and repeatedly attempted to rise, nearly going as far as jumping from the second-floor landing before he was finally restrained by his mother. Reveries of this kind are not, as some would have it, connected to the sexual nature of flying. Though the dream does* appear *to imitate the excitability and anxiety found in the adolescent male, it would be wrong to imagine some bit of poetry here, or worse yet, a symbol. I assert that general biology is the culprit. The quickening of the young male's physiology creates a variety of tremors and flexations in sleep which in turn signal the body that it is in motion—a simple constriction of the bowel can therefore cause a poor boy to take wing.*

My father's journal lies open on the desk beside my own, and there are moments when I take comfort in copying his words, going as far as imitating the low crawl of his script. His thoughts about flying remind me that I am no longer a young man. Instead of rising in dreams, I fall—calamitous head-over-foot plummeting through a hundred ornamented living rooms, nighttime cafés and sweat rich mattresses. I fall through the branches of apple trees. Plunge through oceans, duck ponds, my mother's bath water. I have fallen through glass and fire. Fallen with bombs on spired cities. Fallen away from Amon Garrik a hundred times over again.

It's true that I can no longer recall the expression on the face of my boyhood friend the first time he left the ground. I remember well enough the scene—a sunlit morning. Amon and I were lying in the low hills above my father's stone house, the university a dark island in the distance. Yellow tulips nodded against the verdigris of the hill, and flat-bottomed clouds trundled like hay carts overhead. Bread was baking in the house ovens, and its yeasty scent perfumed the air, mingling with the bright smell of the flowers. Amon was red-cheeked because he'd been in some argument with his father, Helmer Garrik, my own father's rival at the university. Amon thought the whole endeavor of analysis absurd, especially his father's brand—a mythic exploration of man and symbol. "As if the self is a fixed and organized museum," Amon ranted, tearing the head off a tulip and tossing it down the hill. "I can assure you, Roddy, there are no marble hallways in my skull for old men to walk down. No busts of labeled complexes either. Nothing's as pattered as that."

I clasped my fingers behind my head, enjoying the warmth of the sun on my bare arms. "So, what is it you want?" I asked. "For men like our fathers to close shop?

What's the harm in it, Amon? Old men need something to struggle at."

He glared at me. His combination of pale hair and dark eyes could be frightening. "If a pattern doesn't exist, and one continues to search for it, that's mad, isn't it Roddy? And the idea that I am the son of a madman is—" Amon stopped speaking and stood abruptly, as if about to be sick. I thought his tirade might have driven him to dry heaves, but then he made a scrambling motion in the air and lurched forward, stumbling down the hill. Before I could stand to help him, he'd brought his left leg up and didn't bring it down again, as if preparing to mount some invisible staircase. Our stableman was prone to epileptic fits, and on a number of occasions, I'd witnessed his contortions and would have thought the stableman possessed, had my father not been there to explain the illness. I feared one of those fits was taking hold of my friend, but then, without lowering his left foot to the ground, Amon stepped off with his right so that both feet were no longer touching the dewy grass. The clouds ceased their westward trek. The hill was silent.

I've tried to come up with a comparable experience to describe what I witnessed—not only for myself but so I could put it down in this journal—and the only event that comes close to seeing Amon Garrik levitate is seeing my father in his coffin, his body impossibly stiff and painted among the silken folds. The lack of motion in my father's normally animated face was so unbelievable that my mind attempted an adjustment. I actually saw his brow lift, his lips purse because I knew they *must* move. They'd always moved. Likewise, seeing Amon step off the ground and stand in midair, my mind attempted a correction. Such defiance of gravity wasn't possible and therefore I couldn't be seeing it. I imagined the shadow of his boots had taken on some unknown weight and become a part of his foot, that the shadow was, in fact, pushing him off the ground. Then in the next moment, Amon was falling face first into the grass. His face. I try to remember the look on it. Though what, I might ask myself, is so important about remembering an expression? The events that occurred during the months following the day on the hill *should* carry more weight. But without a memory of Amon's expression when he first discovered his miraculous ability, I have no notion of his emotional experience, and it's necessary for me to believe that I *knew* him, both inside and out. The question that I should really put to myself—the more frightening question—is whether I remember Amon's face at all, not the general outline but the specifics of his features. Neither of us had the sort of money necessary to have photographs made, and our warring fathers who daily stepped on one another's egos, would have never loaned us money for such a purpose. I therefore have no visual record of my friend. I tell myself that I *do* remember his face. How could I forget? I begin one attempt at recovery, and then another, until I've made a hundred Amons, each closely resembling the next except for some significant feature, making me believe that none of the boys I've pictured is an accurate representation. I've simply made a desperate series of simulations, only to watch them fall, one by one because they don't live up to my friend's actual presence.

I know he had fine hair on his cheeks which he referred to as his Viking's beard. Amon Garrik was vain about his heritage and refused to trim the growth, though his mother threatened a number of times to do it as he slept and, in the process, to forget to be scrupulous with the razor. Beyond the ruddy down, Amon had a rather plain face, often tanned and primitive, despite the fact that he was the son of an academic. We'd met at a university party, in the dean's torch-lit fall garden—two small men in tailored jackets—and when he introduced himself, I actually laughed.

"What's the joke?" he asked, sharply.

"Your surname," I responded, lips red with punch. "You're Helmer Garrik's son."

"That's right."

"My father pitches the name around our house and shoots at it like a clay pigeon."

"I hate Herr Garrik, too," Amon said, hands folded behind his back, a picture of fastidious organization. "He's a fraud."

"You hate your own father?"

"Of course I do," he said. "Don't you hate yours? I thought that was the modern condition."

I paused, unsure if Amon was making a joke. "He angers me," I said. "But he *is* still my father."

"Does he ask you terrible questions?"

"Terrible?"

The light from the nearest torch played across the damp flagstones between us, drawing us closer as if we were boats on a burning lake. "Embarrassing things," Amon continued. "Sexual fantasies, odd dreams. Just yesterday Herr Garrik asked how I felt about horses. This came out of nowhere during breakfast. I said they were fine though I had no particular interest in them. Then he asked me to *describe* a horse! As if I couldn't."

I search for some correlation from my own experience. "My father once asked me to describe a type of bird, I suppose. I can't remember which. One from America."

Amon's breath smelled of alcohol and cinnamon from his spiced drink. "We could be fast friends, Roddy," he said. "I'm sure of it. We walk a common thread."

For the remainder of the hour, we discussed our fathers' theories, Amon spitting on Herr Garrik's more mystical leanings while I described my father's biological and chemical approach until our mothers came to gather us into waiting cars, not daring to speak or even look at one another. And after that night, Amon and I began to seek each other out, sensing, like animals, if the other was near. Amon's father attributed such ability to an awareness of the Earth's magnetic fields which were said to cover and connect every surface. Some individuals were more attuned to the magnetic fields and could therefore make use of them, pluck them like harp strings.

My father wrote specifically of Amon and me only once, making no reference to Amon's rising. He knew nothing of it at the time. No one did. He wrote: *Neither of the boys has developed symptoms per se, though neurotic illness often cannot be sharply differentiated from health, and the boys are both intelligent enough to fashion a cover. I've heard Helmer Garrik say in one of the follies he calls lectures that inversion has the dynamic characteristics of a dream. The behavior of the invert corresponds to unconscious memory and motivation in the same way that the dream relates to its latent content. A dream of a black dog represents the dreamer's will to power, and the invert's desire for another man represents his inability to process a buried trauma. Here again, I find myself in opposition to Helmer Garrik, but for once, I am also second-guessing my ideas, perhaps because Roderick is involved.*

Helmer Garrik's analysis seems unnecessarily artful—as if he's making an oil painting instead of practicing a science. Black dogs? What use do I have for such poetry? If my son is experiencing amorous desire for his friend, it must be because they share a common trait, chemical or otherwise—they are matched. I have seen the way they lock step and have

*heard a nearly audible note in the air when they catch one
another's glance. It might even be argued that they form a
kind of symmetry when placed side by side. If some yet undiscovered biology is at work, who am I to raise the poetry
of dreams against it?*

I find it strange that Amon and I could have even
appeared symmetrical to an astute outsider such as my
father. If anything, we ruptured symmetry. After the night
in the burning garden we became almost immediately
and unthinkingly physical. There was nothing we would
not attempt in the deserted barns and forest clearings
around the university. We developed a certain mania in
each other's presence, breaking from our learned structures and tearing at each other, biting and pushing until
we were each spent, and then just as quickly going at it
again. It seems foolish for me, an old man, to sit and recall
these pleasures and nearly as obscene for me to write them
down in detail, especially when, quite possibly, someone
will read this piece of writing, as I've been reading my
own father's journals. What could I hope to gain by setting
down the specifics of my entanglements with Amon? Joy
recollected is indeed no longer the emotion itself. Nor is
lust. Nor passion. Suffice it to say we were not gentle with
each other. When we wanted to call out and draw attention
to ourselves, we instead bit into one another's flesh.

After that day in the hills when Amon inexplicably
stepped into the air, we were distracted from our bodies
and drew closer because of it. We ran experiments, having learned inductive reasoning from our fathers, and attempted to recreate the circumstances that led to Amon's
"miracle." We added and subtracted elements but never
found the desired effect. Amon was unable to climb off
the ground even an inch. He punched hay bales in our

barn from frustration until his knuckles were bloodied, and the stableman had to wrap them.

I pointed out that it might have been Amon's anger at his father that day which produced the effect, and so he attempted to conjure similar feelings the next windy day on the hill—to enlarge himself like a sail with his emotions. Still nothing came of it. He worried it might have been a specific quality of anger that could not simply be reproduced via force of will, but I persuaded him against such a theory. Amon was an emotional person and there were days he vented continually, cycling through entire operas of sorrow and rage. Certainly, he would have landed on the right formulation in all of that.

He wanted to leap off the cliff that overlooked the river in an attempt to force a reoccurrence, but I wouldn't allow it, arguing the jump met too few of the requirements necessary for recreation, and there were sharp rocks in the river, only one of which would need to make contact with his skull in order to ensure that he never rose again.

I suppose it could be argued that I intentionally sabotaged these experiments, fearing that a repeat of Amon's levitation would draw a line between us. He would go where I could not follow, and I couldn't bear that. I'd only recently found him and needed to keep us both on the ground.

One night, after weeks of discrete satisfaction, I heard a tapping on my window glass. My bedroom was on the second floor of our stone house, and the tapping roused me from sleep. Perhaps still half inside a dream, I pictured a grotesque bird outside my window with claws on the tips of its wings, scales on its chest, and Amon's head sewn to its neck. The thread was drawn taught against his skin and caused it to pucker in places so his flesh gaped. I could see through to the dark inner-body beneath. The abomination leered at me through the drapery, and when

I realized that the vision was not entirely a product of my dreaming, I jumped from my bed, shaken. Amon was actually outside my second-story window, though of course he hadn't become half bird. His body was as solid and consistent as ever, and for once he seemed pleased. I pulled open the window and glanced downward, sickened by the height and the possibility of a fall, but Amon stood midair without fear, boot heels locked, hands clasped behind his back. "Good evening, Roddy," he said. "I thought you might be lonely."

"How—" I answered, unable to find the necessary words to complete my thought.

"Not sure, actually. Would you like to come out and try?" I recoiled, but his hand was already on my wrist. A scream would have raised the household, particularly my father, a light sleeper, so I allowed him to pull me. Amon wasn't gentle. He jerked my body over the windowpane, ensuring that I could no longer hold my balance. Then using all of his force, he lifted me until I was standing barefoot on his muddied boots, both his arms around me. The sensation of hanging in the air with him was dizzying, and my mind scrambled for some purchase in the rational. "You see?" he said. "It isn't death. I have enough lift for both of us."

"Amon," I begged. "Put me back. You don't know how you did this. You don't know how long it will last."

"It's different this time, Roddy," he said, as he carefully undid the string of my nightshirt and let it flutter to the dark hedges below. "I can sense it."

I could sense it too. I felt my chest fill with stars. My spine bent against the moon. Amon continued to smile as he kissed the hollow of my neck. We made a careful love that night, not as fierce as our previous endeavors. Perhaps it was because he had to keep both hands on me, and I had to remain standing upon his boots. Or maybe our tenderness was due to the fact that his hovering in the air seemed a kind of rite. We knew better than to defile it. Watching my nightshirt flutter in the shrubbery below, I remember thinking I had received my own understanding of the universe's magnificent pattern, one that could finally usurp my father's.

So began Amon Garrik's nightly visits to the stone house. He would lift me from my window frame as one would lift a doll from its dollhouse. I rarely slept, as sleep was no longer a worthy experience. My parents became concerned about the shadows pooled in my face, and I learned to use my mother's powder to cover the darkness beneath my eyes. Amon was learning too—not only to hover in the sky but to walk clumsily, and I walked with him, standing on his boots, facing forward, his hands around my abdomen. We trudged through the night as if stepping through piles of invisible snow, and there was nothing as wonderful as the sensation of tilting with him over an abyss, though of course the abyss was nothing more than my father's yew bushes and the duck pond with its crowd of decorative French angels.

Then after nearly a month of these sky walks, there was a night when Amon didn't arrive, and I sat in my nest of sheets until the sun crested the low hills, bringing with it a confirmation of what I feared. Amon's rising had finally taken him somewhere I could not go. He'd realized that such power was enough in itself, and there was no reason for him to drag me along, to be hindered by my weight. I dressed hastily and ran to the road that led to the Garrik house, fighting tears and wondering what I might say when Frau Garrik answered the door.

In a tall patch of weeds, I found him, shirtless and wearing only one boot. His ruddy hair stood on end, and his skin was streaked with chimney soot. Most troublingly, Amon no longer looked exactly like the boy I knew. It was some other creature I found burning in the button weeds. His body appeared hollow and weightless, as if a strong wind might lift him back to the sky at any moment. I shook Amon, fearing the worst, and when he opened his eyes, I realized how truly different he was. The world inside him had become larger than the world without. There was a whole landscape in his eyes, and a secondary sun hung in his sky. I was but an insect on a branch in that world. "Roddy—" his tongue was salty white. "Something incredible—"

I didn't want to know. I feared knowing. "I thought you were dead, Amon."

"It was a sort of death," he whispered.

"No poetry," I said.

He raised himself in the button weeds, and I saw how difficult it was for him to move upon the earth. The gravity irritated him, as he no longer belonged to it. "Listen to me," he said. "I started out as I always do, taking small steps, intending to make my way to your window, and then I caught a glimpse of something different. There were tears in my eyes from the cold wind. Maybe they were enough for me to see—"

"See what?"

"Our fathers are correct, Roddy, though neither one of the old men knows how right they actually are. There *is* a pattern. But it isn't one of myth or science. I caught a glimpse of it in the air. Something beyond our fathers' imaginings, a glittering and navigable geometry that covers everything and passes *through* everything. Cords of light, braces of gold. I learned to make use of them last night. I actually flew, Roddy. No more toddling along like a baby. And the faster I flew, the brighter the pattern appeared to me, until I realized there were animals with me in the sky, making use of the pattern—not birds or bats, but bright bodies with tremendous faces—things that might have once been mistaken for gods. *I* almost mistook them for that at first, but then I realized they were like me. Beings who'd recognized the great geometry."

"You flew with these *things?*" I said, trying to picture the monsters.

"I'll take you," he said. "Tonight, I'll take you."

"I don't want to go, Amon."

He burst into laughter. "Don't want to go?" he said, grabbing me roughly by the arm as he used to. "We'll speak to them together. I was *waiting* for you. Maybe they can tell us how to stay permanently in the sky. To live there as they do. We wouldn't have to worry about hiding ourselves."

"You can't fly," I said.

His god-face broke with surprise. "What?"

"I don't believe you," I said. "I don't *have* to believe you. I think you just went off and did what you wanted. Maybe you went spying on girls in town, and now you're making up a story to frighten me. There are no things with tremendous faces that live in the sky. Come on, Amon. I've been educated."

As if to prove me wrong, Amon reached into the air, grabbed hold of some object I couldn't see, and lifted himself off the ground, floating effortlessly up for a moment and then dropping gently back to his feet. I shut my eyes. I would not see a thing like that. Not anymore. Storming away, heedless of the holes in the road, I left him to his madness. For it was madness, and I knew the moment that either of our fathers saw him, he'd be immediately diagnosed. He could not conceal it any longer, not when his eyes looked as they did, so full of nauseating space. He'd be taken to the clinic and studied. When our fathers spoke of underlying patterns, they didn't mean glittering architectures. They simply meant underlying principles of organization. But nothing Amon said was organized or logical. Did I believe him about the events of the previous night? I suppose on some level, I did, yet my mind continued its attempts at rationalization. I didn't want his truths.

That night when he came tapping, I hid beneath my covers and forced him to call through the thick glass, begging me to unlock the window. I should have gone to him when he said he was afraid to travel again in the night alone, but I didn't. Eventually, he left, and I wish that I'd at least looked out to see him strong and mad one last time. I wish I'd memorized him, laid him out in a high garden somewhere in my mind.

Should I say it came as a surprise when I descended from my room the next morning and found my mother and father sitting at our formal table with Helmer Garrik and his wife, dressed in dark clothes, a bowl of yellow flowers from the hill between them. I immediately believed that Amon and I had been found out, that we were being officially labeled by our fathers as inverts. We'd be separated and given the talking cure for months. I went to my mother and put my face on her shoulder.

"The Garriks are here," my father began, "because of a terrible event that befell their son, Amon, on our property last night."

"An event?" I said.

Frau Garrik took hold of her husband's hand. "Your stableman," she said, biting the tips off her words, "he shot our boy. Shot our beautiful boy in the head last night."

The breakfast parlor began to dissolve. No parents. No careful tea. Only a rash of yellow on an otherwise empty canvas.

When I struck the floor, I was surprised, having always believed I would fall when I was *with* Amon. But there was no truth to this. I fell without him. My father gathered me in his arms, and I looked up into the sharp bristles of his mustache, the holes of his nostrils. He was himself a pit of some depth. "The stableman must have been having one of his fits," he said quietly. "They're known to cause dementia, though I certainly wasn't aware of the extent to which he suffered. He's been telling us all morning that he didn't shoot a boy, didn't shoot Amon. He says he shot a large bird or even a kind of dragon out of the sky.

Frau Garrik broke down in wrenching sobs, and Helmer Garrik began calling to me in his stony voice, asking if I understood why his son might have been on our property at midnight, or why he might have been mistaken for a dragon, of all things. My father didn't allow me time to answer. Instead he carried me up the stairs, telling me I must rest.

I told him I couldn't. I'd never rest after this, and he closed the door of my bedroom, taking a seat at the foot of my bed. My father looked like an old man in that moment, his silk vest stretched tightly across his paunch, the hair on the top of his head so fine it was nearly invisible in the morning light. He watched his hands as he spoke. "You cared for him, Roderick?"

"I did," I said, unable to restrain myself. "Very much."

He nodded, speaking slowly and with care. "In the war, there was a custom. We wrote letters to the dead. Placed them in the coffin near the hands so they might be opened, even in darkness. You'll write a letter. Tell Amon how you felt. But you'll tell no one else. Do you understand me?"

"Yes."

"Herr Garrik wants me to bring you to the clinic for a stay. I don't know that I can refuse him after what's happened."

I put my face in my father's hands, felt his warmth, rested.

I've searched for some final passage from his professional journal to finish this, wanting to close with a sense of symmetry. But there are no further passages about flight, and my father certainly wrote nothing else about me. After the events of that day, he was careful to exclude me from his studies. I can almost feel my father next to me as I write this, or perhaps it's that he is a part of me. The Garriks wouldn't allow me to attend Amon's funeral, and when I nearly went mad from this, my father told me what to do. I burned the letter I wrote to Amon Garrik on the hill among the yellow tulips where he first stepped into the air, and as the smoke of my words rose into the clear sky above, I imagined the bright animals with their tremendous faces, somehow reaching down and finding a way to accept those ashes as offering.

A Man of History

TO BECOME HIS BELOVED FRIEND, his minion, as it were; to
stand at his side; wear the same flower; sleep in the same
bed—all of this he wanted, and yet even before I took up
rooms with him, I think Thomas Weymouth understood
the impossibility of our union. Perhaps he'd even predicted
our parting the moment we met; there was something in
his expression at the gallery—a future sadness, a telescop-
ing of years. I was freshly graduated, touring the British
Museum in a ridiculous velvet jacket; my hair inspired perhaps by Rimbaud. I'd lost my friend Marie near Raphael's
Madonna of the Pinks (one of her favorites—a work she said
she could make a life inside of) and had wandered into
another set of cold rooms where I attempted to analyze a
Flemish portrait of Sir Philip the Good for the benefit of a
complete stranger, an older man in an antique robe and
formless hat who'd caught my attention.

It was my habit in those days to strike up conversation with anyone of interest, especially those of a dramatic

air. I liked the dolor of the older man's face, the deep-set nature of his eyes. His clothes seemed to absorb the gallery light, and though he was not a man of fashion, the whole room seemed to bend to his gravity. I pointed to the oil on canvas and said wasn't it interesting how Philip the Good's melancholic expression likened him to a medieval city; he was girded by his despair, a self-sufficient microcosm who needed nothing and wanted less. The unknown Flemish painter had captured the self-reliance in the subject's hooded eyes and the ramparts of his cheekbones. Or was it self-reliance? Perhaps isolation was something forced upon him. As with all people who are truly *good*, I continued, there seemed a barrier between Sir Philip and the world. He retained virtue through seclusion, never venturing into the dark woods beyond his walls.

Lord Weymouth, the stranger's title I'd later learn, half-smiled as he listened, hands tucked in the sleeves of his odd robe. He gently reminded me that Philip the Good was known to have had a congenital illness which might account for hooded eyes and melancholic mood, but he was also quick to add that he preferred my poetic sense to any such grim reality. "An artful description not only of loneliness," he said, "but of its physical deformations."

I attempted to catch sight of Marie's pagoda sleeves and pastel skirts. "Are you a Medievalist then?" I asked, intending to excuse myself after he answered.

"Hardly an academic," he replied. "But men with money have time to linger. Endless hours of repose. I'm sure you've read about it."

I glanced at the gentleman's hand. He wore a heavy ring—not a wedding ring but an artifact, and I wondered despite myself who he might be. It wasn't as though I was a fortune hunter, but I was wise enough to know that a young man without options should remain alert. It was fashionable at the time to play Greek after graduating without coming to abominate, of course.

"I'm in possession of a text which may be of some interest to a student," he continued.

"A student of finance?" I asked, having earned such a degree, which Marie and I were expecting to celebrate that night.

For a moment, actual amusement lightened his heavy face, transforming him from the memento mori he had been. "It's worth a great deal, I suppose," he said. "Though I'd never sell it. It's quite dear to me—the diary of a knight errant and his squire. I rescued it from a disreputable dealer."

"You bought it on the black market?"

"Rescued," he corrected.

"Very like a knight then," I said. "Courage, honor, and endless self-delusion."

He lifted the sleeve of his robe to his mouth and coughed. "You must be a student of psychology as well."

"Kenton Sands," I said, extending my hand. "Incorrigible generalist."

He neither shook my hand nor introduced himself, and I'd later learn from his servant, Mrs. Philips, that going to the museum and inspecting the Medieval artifacts was one of the few excursions Lord Weymouth allowed himself. He was not adept at *meeting* and became terribly uncomfortable around new faces that were not done in oil and brushstroke. "It's the diary of Sir Stephen de Lorris," he said. "Sir Stephen of Sorrows. It's as strange an account as I've ever read from the period. There are a few adventures and then the whole thing takes a frightening turn."

"Frightening how?" I asked, tucking my untouched hand into the pocket of my velvet jacket and feeling the edge of Marie's lace handkerchief which she'd given me earlier that day to blot perspiration. I'd begun having small attacks since my graduation—panic really—a throat-closing, hand-numbing feeling because I'd been cast out of a system I dearly loved. I was free-falling in the world of commerce. And I realized I hadn't excused myself as I'd intended, but there was nothing wolfish about the man. He was neither superior nor predatory. Instead he was lonely and trying his best to make conversation—on top of that, he was succeeding at holding my interest.

"My knight discovers how time betrays love," he said. "The specifics of the story you'd have to come hear for yourself."

"I'm afraid I can't. I have to locate my friend," I said.

He drew himself slightly taller and the gold-framed paintings seemed to swim around him in the dim gallery light—all those pallid men and women, sitting for their portraits—stags and oceans, skulls and fields of wheat. "I assure you, Kenton Sands, that you will find these artifacts more interesting than any modern friend. Despite your attempts to hide it, you seem a man of history."

*

FROM THE MUSEUM, we took dinner of stewed turtle and red wine at the Winged Stag, apparently a favorite of Lord Weymouth and then continued on to his home, called Longleat House, which was not as impressive as I'd imagined. Rather forlorn-looking with its black-painted shutters and slouching porch, it stood on the outskirts of the fashionable neighborhood of Mayfair. From a locked cabinet (one of many in the house), he produced the diary, a copy of a copy bound between boards and covered in cracked leather. It bore what he told me was the blazon of Sir Stephen de Lorris—a St. Andrew's cross. "Unlike Christ," Lord Weymouth said, touching the embossment, "St. Andrew was crucified on the diagonal—his cross in the shape of an X, you see. I think my knight identified with such a death. Out of kilter. Ready to fall off the edge of the Earth at any moment."

"May I have a look?" I asked. Lord Weymouth treated the book with such totemic reverence that I felt the need to touch the thing myself if only to prove it did not burn in my hand.

He pulled away. "I'll read aloud to you, Mr. Sands," he said, "if you don't mind."

Who was I to argue? I had no governance in his home. The trip to Longleat had been a lark and, in my mind, remained so. I wondered about Marie—walking the chilly galleries alone, perhaps skulking around the Elgin Marbles waiting for some direction from their pale blank eyes. I might catch up with her in a few hours, I thought, but as soon as we'd settled by the fire and were served brandy by the servant, Mrs. Philips, I forgot the world outside. Lord Weymouth opened his book and situated it in his lap so I could not see the lettering, and I half-closed my eyes to enjoy the narrative.

What did he read to me that first evening? I want to say it was the story of how Sir Stephen de Lorris met his squire, Pieter, in the woods after competing in an allegory held by the Duchess of Burgundy. This, after all, was the day that would forever change Sir Stephen's life, and it would make for a logical introduction to his tale. Not only did he meet Pieter, but he won the Burning Armor as a result of freeing a so-called giant from the gilded oak in the center of the battlefield. The Duchess was known to have become involved in alchemy after the death of her husband, an event which had freed her from wifely constraints, and the Burning Armor was purportedly a product of her arts.

71

Its mysterious sheen of reddish gold that appeared almost alive did not belie such rumors.

But in truth, the Duchess was more actress than alchemist. The giant was nothing more than a slightly taller than normal man guarded by dwarves, and the gilded oak had been painted earlier that morning so it glittered as if from Avalon. An allegory or a masque as they were sometimes known, according to Lord Weymouth, was a piece of theater—a stylized tournament held during the age of Elizabeth. There were actors dressed as gods and goddesses—the Duchess herself was arrayed as gray-eyed Athena, carrying shield and olive branch, and Pieter portrayed a lesser deity, Anteros, who stood for requited love, the sort that is fulfilling and good and does not lead to a life of longing. There were, as well, actual knights taking part in the allegory, mostly lower-class men, all vying for the prized armor and a few words with the Duchess.

Pieter as Anteros wore sleeves of crow feathers and painted his torso with lead and vinegar so he shone brightly in the sun. When Sir Stephen saw the young man for the first time, he stopped his fight and stood frozen, the chambers of his heart flooding with icy water as if a winter dam had burst. He thought something had gone awry at the Duchess's allegory and in fact a truth had risen from her artifice. Was it possible that, as in ancient times, a god was paying visit to the world of men? "Wait there," he managed to say to Pieter over the noise of the brawl. "Come tell me your name."

Startled because knights were not permitted to talk to the actors at the allegory, as such distraction would pierce the Duchess's carefully planned illusion, Pieter ran off across the battlefield to gather with the other lesser gods. And for the rest of the tournament, Sir Stephen searched for the young man—a pagan flower blooming on the icy banks of his humble Christian heart.

But I think it was not this passage that Lord Weymouth chose to read that night. It would have been too obvious, perhaps, after our own meeting at the museum. "Wait there...come tell me who you are," was the command hanging in the air whether we heard Sir Stephen speak it or not. Lord Weymouth gauged my reaction to his story, glancing up from the page from time to time. He may have read a passage closer to the end of Sir Stephen's life. After Pieter had been killed at the Battle of Novara where Sir Stephen had been attempting to make a name for himself, the knight retreated in despair and burrowed alone in the tower of a flooded castle near a lake in Glastonbury, writing lines of poetry to his lost squire. Lord Weymouth read with deep compassion: "I could not keep myself from your hair—pulling at it and twisting it to make tendrils of flame. My hands ache for you. The centers of my palms. Fine straight nose, cleft of chin, tiny ears tucked close to the head. Where has all this glamour gone? The forehead has broken, hair turned gray and lashes come off. The eyes themselves are tarnished mirror glass, and who am I but a man of vanity left to sit and look?"

The Burning Armor was laid out on Sir Stephen's table like a permanent funeral or a feast, never to be eaten. There was a hole in the suit of armor's side, still ringed with Pieter's own blood. The young man had been wearing the plating when he died at Novara, running ahead foolishly as if at sport. He and Sir Stephen were boys playing at war, and even when Pieter fell on an idle spear, driving the head through the weak metal, he looked at it with surprise, as if he could brush the shaft away and go on. Sir Stephen stripped off his own gloves and held Pieter's head. "The Burning Armor," Pieter whispered, grimacing at the pain, "how could it not save me?"

Without money or honor, Sir Stephen retired. Peasants from Glastonbury threw stones at his turret. He prayed for a *danse macabre*—for Pieter to pull himself from his grave all in silver and wings of black as he'd been on the day of their first meeting. He wished the squire would drag him to the underworld by the hair, asking why Sir Stephen had allowed such a death, begging with a throat full of dirt to know what sort of knight allowed his good helpmate to be erased, swept off into the circling ether? Weren't they supposed to be printed together in the histories?

My first evening at Longleat ended in drunkenness from the ever full cup of brandy, and I fell asleep in my chair by the fire, somehow already unafraid of Lord Weymouth. When the embers in the hearth had gone white, Mrs. Philips came to cover me with a woolen blanket, tucking it around the edges of my body, and in a dream, I saw Sir Stephen and his squire, Pieter, fording a stream—the trees around them glittered with pastoral light. The stream itself was carved glass laid in the woods. And the two men were laughing. Pieter carried the Burning Armor on his back. His reddish-blond hair matched the color of the metal so perfectly. Sir Stephen wore a sun coat made of silk, the blazon of Saint Andrew on his chest, and the X of that cross looked like a mark or a target. Was I foolish enough to think I could join them? Walk along their trail and laugh with them? The two men heard my movements in the woods. I'd stepped on a branch and they turned to look, searching for me, the dreamer, and when they found my hiding place, their eyes were not as kindly as I'd imagined. They were not eyes at all, in fact, but holes dug into the earth. Ragged pits with stony sides. And in those holes were animals, bone-thin and starving, caveish and so fearful of the light.

A Man of History

*

LORD WEYMOUTH KNEW that I would leave London. He said he could see in the plainness of my face that I was set on moving to some suburb, Maiden Bradley or another like it, taking up with a wife and using my degree to become a clerk. "The velvet coats and poet's hair don't fool me, dear boy, but you might as well stay for a bit. Work at Longleat. I have certain finances that need looking after." He must have known a part of me would remain—even if I declined the work and chose to take my leave at that moment. Perhaps he could see the dream of Sir Stephen in me or that my heart too was a ruin, one that the suburbs would not restore. I would visit him at Christmastime, bring fruit and sit with him as one would sit with a father. We had a future together, and even if it was not precisely the one he desired, Lord Weymouth had learned to settle.

The summer I made my home at Longleat was a dark one. Storm clouds rose like castle walls at the edges of the city, and each day brought with it some new difficulty. There was the question of where I should sleep. Mrs. Philips had prepared a room, but Lord Weymouth insisted that I take the spare bed in his own chamber, so we might talk well into the night. He stayed up late telling me stories of Sir Stephen, instances he recalled from the diary. Sir Stephen and Pieter had briefly joined in the search for the Grail; they'd been taken aboard a ship of plague victims and narrowly escaped through the cunning of Pieter who'd fashioned a rowboat from barrel sides; they'd found what they believed to be the tomb of Lancelot in a quiet grove and had knelt to pray to him as if he were a god, and on and on. Then there was my friend Marie, who wanted to visit, an event which Lord Weymouth forbade, saying he could not stand the thought of her childish laughter ringing in his house. He did not like me to go to the taverns or even to the museums. His moods became excruciating—roses of anger blooming his cheeks. A man who'd lived alone for so long had no business inviting someone to lodge at his home. He would leave the supper table, knocking his plate to the floor if I made a misstep in etiquette. He would chastise me if I left for my morning constitution without saying goodbye. Lord Weymouth was dragged beneath waves of poetry and despair, turning again and again to Sir Stephen and Pieter and entreating me to sit and listen, as if some education were taking place. On certain days, his sadness became a ceiling, and Mrs. Philips and I labored beneath the weight of it.

"When a man puts so much stock in a book of history," Mrs. Philips said to me one afternoon over the remnants of a late tea, "that he begins to *live* in that other time, we must wonder what is missing from his life. I do feel sorry for my Lord, Mr. Sands. But you have brought some light to him. You should have seen this place before you came. There were months when he would not let me touch a thing—the sound of cleaning was too much for him, he said. It disrupted his reading. So much the better to have you walking these halls instead of the ghosts of that awful knight and his boy."

It would be vanity to say I was the only cause for Lord Weymouth's despair. There must have been other men—a whole life of them perhaps that led to his obsession with the fantastic and useless diary of Sir Stephen. Mrs. Philips must have known about these men, of course, but she was the kind of woman who tended to let such details slip beneath her fastidiously pressed tablecloths. There were times when I thought she'd drifted as deep into a state of fantasy as he, eternally adjusting her gray uniform, acting as though at any moment "her Lord" might announce that he'd finally decided on a wife.

"Our late age," Lord Weymouth told me during one of his moments of clarity, "is devoted almost entirely to acting out the vision of a dream. Each of us has his own. I have my knight and you have your future happy home in the suburb. Even Mrs. Philips has a dream, I suppose. A dust-free countertop, perhaps. But collectively those dreams become *phenomena*—a definition of the age. What would Victoria think of all this dreaming—her subjects crawling through the bracken, mere animals attempting to achieve the sublime?"

I left him after a single summer. Three months in all. He offered to hire me permanently as his financier, though by that time I'd already discovered there were no finances to speak of. The house of Weymouth was bankrupt and had been for some one hundred years. I took my leave of Longleat under poorer circumstances than when I'd arrived, no longer able to withstand even a moment of Lord Weymouth's fantasies of the knight.

"You're mad," I said to him in the darkness of our bed chamber. "You and Mrs. Philips live inside this hospital and support each other's sickness."

"Are you the sane one then, Kenton?" he asked, voice a quiet growl. "Are you the doctor who's come to take our temperatures?"

We argued on the evening of my departure—I don't remember the subject. Mrs. Philips wept as if she were losing a son, but as I've said already, I did not stay away for long. I returned at least once a month until my marriage—dragged back by some compulsion. Then my visits became rarer—so rare, in fact, that excursions to Longleat took on a significance larger than themselves. Visits crystallized into symbol: a return to youth. I was pleased to remember that time of confusion—the drama of my poet's heart. Ascending the high steps to the door lit by street-lamps and gazing through the leaded glass at a distortion of the marbled foyer, I felt a warmth that my home in Maiden Bradley could not provide. The humble door opened even before my hand had touched the knocker, and it was as if I was folding myself back into reverie. Life in the suburbs was no longer my dream. Instead, my summer at Long-leat called to me. The shabby rooms of Weymouth and the violence of its Lord had been trimmed to fit my foolish reach for the sublime.

Each time Mrs. Philips escorted me down the hall to the room where Lord Weymouth sat by his fire, facing an empty chair, I felt years slip away. It was a pleasure to hear her chat happily about recent events in their lives—what few events there were. I was once again a boy of eighteen, marveling at the glass cases of Medieval artifacts. One shelf alone held the fang of the mythic boar of Garin, a Psalter used by St. Louis, and a bizarre statue of the Vir-gin, hinged so it could open and reveal a trinity within her womb. Mother Mary was prepared to give birth not only to a boy-child but an angry-looking god and a white dove with beams of light blazing from its skull.

In greeting Lord Weymouth, I watched for intrusions of age, some intimation that these visits would not continue. My own father had died during my youth, and since then I waited constantly for the expiration of older men. I stud-ied Lord Weymouth as he stood to welcome me, watching for a wince of arthritis or a foot askew—a furtherance of slippage and of loss. Yet such changes were infrequent. He seemed the same man, unhappy, yes, but in good health. I began to wonder if by returning to Longleat I was keeping him in some stasis. He did not change, because I did not. I was still the young graduate come to hear his stories—and there were always more of those. Stories of how Pieter was enchanted by a castle of maidens and Sir Stephen had to rescue him in the night. Of how they found the mythic pool of Narcissus and discovered that the boy's spirit still floated on the surface of that water. Or how they discovered a dark nest hanging from a tree in the forest, and they pulled at it and pierced it with their swords until they realized it was the Earth's sadness—a tumescent growth and there was no way to heal a thing like that.

It was not until my final visit at Longleat—the last time I saw Lord Weymouth—that I realized how much he'd changed over those years, all the while covering it with a mask. When I attempt to describe our last evening, I find myself losing word and audience. My wife, a good example, will not listen. She adopts an uncharacteristically hazy expression, as if looking at a shape in the far distance, beyond what she can see clearly. She shuts the windows behind her eyes. My mother used to wear such a face when kneading bread dough. In the happy light in our stone kitchen near Avon, she pulled at the floured meal, working her fingers and eventually allowing her entire body to sway, all the while looking as if she were watching something invisible and far off. When I asked what she saw, what she fixed her eyes upon, she laughed and said, "What a ridiculous question Kenton—I don't see anything but the kitchen—I know it all too well." But I persisted, and finally she said that if she had to give an answer, she would tell me that she imagined her fingers were dissolving in the dough. This was something she'd thought about since she was a child. She tried to relay this with laughter, but I could tell she didn't find it funny. The longer she kneaded the dough, the more it seemed as though her fingers were extending into the tensile compound and dissolving. Eventually, when she was well into her work, she had no hands at all.

THIS **NEW** & **POISONOUS AIR**

An attempt to write down what I experienced that Christmas Eve is perhaps an attempt to literalize—to make physical a thing which was not. And yet what more can I do? Like my mother, I must have hands. I must pull back from my kneading and see my fingers whole again. Now that Lord Weymouth is gone, I must ensure I do not follow him down that strange path. I must know the footing, recognize where the groundwork begins.

*

IT WAS MY WIFE AMELIA'S IDEA to go into the city. She wanted to finish up her Christmas shopping, and I asked if it might be all right for me to pay a visit to Lord Weymouth while she went to Bainbridge's, one of the city's voluminous new department stores, claiming to support a living miniature of London within its walls. Anything that could be bought elsewhere could also be bought at Bainbridge's, and the thought of the place was dreadful. Lord Weymouth himself said it had more levels than Dante's *Purgatorio* and *Inferno* combined and such a place was to be avoided. Amelia agreed to my visit, having no interest in shopping with me. Nor did she have qualms with Lord Weymouth, unaware of his propensities and pleased that he'd kept me from my friend Marie all those summers ago. The two of us parted ways in Piccadilly, and I traveled in the rocking carriage down snow-laden streets toward Longleat, thinking not of Lord Weymouth but of Sir Stephen de Lorris. I was surprised at how often I became caught in those stories, thinking about the long-dead man. For most of the journal, the knight errant was without winters, living in some eternal spring and summer with Pieter. I had become like Lord Weymouth, taking pleasure in simply recounting their early adventures to myself because they spoke to a rarely seen kindness of life.

A Man of History

Even before I reached the door of Longleat that Christmas Eve, I realized something was wrong. The lamps in the entry were not lit nor any of those in the front windows. At first, I feared Lord Weymouth might have left the place—unlikely though that seemed since Longleat was his ancestral home. Rather than having the door open before my first knocking, I had to rap three or four times in order to draw response, and when Mrs. Philips *did* come, she was in terrible disarray. Her uniform looked as if it had not been pressed and her white hair had fallen around her face. "Oh, Mr. Sands," she said. I felt that I should grab hold of her because she looked like she might fall, but instead I took her hand which seemed to rouse her a bit. "What is it?" I asked. "Is Lord Weymouth alright?"

"No. Not alright," she said. "Not at all."

I stepped across the threshold into the darkness of the house. "Go slow now, dear. Tell me what's happened."

She seemed to catch her fear for a moment so she could talk. "There was another young man a few weeks ago. From the museum. He looked so much like you, Mr. Sands, I thought he would be kind, but he was not. He accused Lord Weymouth of terrible things. He took his accusations to the constable."

I stood frozen.

"They came not more than a day ago. They're going to come again after Christmas, and I fear they may take him. He told me I should pack my things in case of that event. And I said, pack my things? How should I pack an entire room? Put my whole life in luggage? But what could this young man have accused him of? Lord Weymouth never hurt you, did he, Mr. Sands?"

I wanted to comfort her, but after looking at her pink and tear-swollen face, I felt not compassion but anger.

"Please, Mrs. Philips, don't play-act. It won't do any good. You know very well what he's being accused of."

She shook her head, folding her arms over her apron and looking as if she was going to cry. When I did not respond to her condition, she said, "You'll help him, won't you, Kenton? He's not strong, nor am I. We can't be taken from Longleat. And you're a man of learning. You have good standing. You can help, can't you? I was hoping you'd come." Instead of responding with further unkind words, I asked her to take me to him, but she didn't move. "There is something else," she said, and the dark hallway felt terribly cold—the house utterly silent, but for our voices.

"What *else* could there be?" I asked.

"A box," she said. "A large crate. It arrived special delivery this morning, and he's been sitting in his room all day staring at it. He hasn't spoken to me. Hasn't touched food. He only looks at the box."

"He hasn't opened it?"

"No, sir. But I believe it to contain something in regards to the knight. Sir Stephen is the only thing that makes my Lord behave in such odd ways."

I took her arm. "I want you to go to your room and remain there," I said. "Have a cup of tea as we used to do. Read a book that soothes your nerves."

"And you'll help him? You'll help us?"

"I will."

She hurried off into the shadows, and I adjusted my coat before walking firmly down the hall toward the parlor, putting one foot in front of the next, attempting to decide what I could possibly say to Lord Weymouth. I certainly couldn't *help* him. The penalties for his sort of crimes grew more stringent by the year, and coercing a younger man into such a life would be punished dearly. He hadn't coerced me of course; we'd colluded, I suppose, though there had been nothing physical about the thing. Our connection had been played out through Sir Stephen, stories of Romance and passion played out on the page, reveled in by both of us. And yet I had been able to remove myself; all the more reason I could not become entangled in any legalities concerning Lord Weymouth's life at the museum.

I entered the room, expecting to find a man beside himself with anxiety, but what I saw was Lord Weymouth dressed comfortably and sitting by a low fire. The lights in the parlor were out as they were everywhere else in the house, but the firelight revealed the shaded hollows of his face and that his hair had changed color since last I'd seen him, turning to spun silver. In his lap he held the diary of Sir Stephen, the blazon gleaming on its cover, and near the chair was the crate Mrs. Philips had described—large enough to hold a bank safe. He squinted at me for a moment, as if he'd lost his eyesight too, then said, "Ah, Kenton. Come to wish me a fine Christmas?"

I approached his chair, wondering if I should play along with his greeting. Instead, I replied with, "Mrs. Philips told me what's happened."

"Many things," he said, sighing. "Many things have happened."

"Do you have money for a barrister?"

He raised his woolish eyebrows. "Whatever would I need a barrister for?"

"Because you will be taken to court and given a rough trial," I said. "A barrister might be able to reduce the length of sentence. I know a few men in Maiden Bradley. I could ask them if—"

He waved his hand. "No need for all that trouble, Kenton," he said. "But I *am* glad you're here." He looked at me carefully, and there was a pinched expression on his face that I'd never seen before, as if there were a straight pin sticking him from the cushion of his chair. "I want you to take Sir Stephen's diary," he told me.

"I couldn't do that," I replied. "Lord Weymouth, I couldn't."

But he was already attempting to hand it to me, and in his weakness, he dropped it to the floor. The book fell open, revealing its pages to me for the first time, and we both stared down at the stark whiteness of them, utterly blank. It was a journal of some sort, made to look antique, but certainly it had never belonged to a Medieval knight. It was the sort of thing that could be bought at Bainbridge's. I quickly gathered the book and closed it, putting it beneath my coat. "I'll take the diary," I said. "I'll keep it safe in the suburbs."

Lord Weymouth laughed. "What would Sir Stephen and Pieter make of the suburbs?" he said.

"I'm sure they'd find adventures there," I replied. "Now please, we should talk seriously for a moment about your plan."

He took a deep breath. "I don't need the book anymore," he said, "because I have *that*." He gestured to the wooden crate sitting near the fire. "Each of us, Kenton, is building a collection in life, piece by meager piece. There are many men who do not realize what they seek and would not even know how to look for a capstone—an object that completes the collection. You, for instance—what do you collect?"

I thought of my home in Maiden Bradley. I'd collected nothing in those rooms; Amelia had made most of the decorations.

"What's the capstone?" I said.

"I'd been tracking it for nearly a year," he replied. "It surfaced at a Turkish bazaar, believe it or not. A collector there purchased it and knowing of my interest, contacted me. I had to give him most of my artifacts in trade just to acquire this piece, but it completes the story after all. It's necessary."

"What?" I said. "What completes the story?"

He put his hand on his brow, as if even the dim light from the fire were too much for him. "The Burning Armor," he said softly. "Both their skins, Sir Stephen's and Pieter's, will have been inside it. There could be remnants of the boy's blood even. It is there inside that crate. And here I sit too frightened to open the thing. Aren't I a ridiculous old man, Kenton?"

"No," I said. "No, you're not. But Lord Weymouth— Thomas, the book—"

"Yes," he said. "You'll take the book. I know all the stories by heart. And at any rate, I will have the men themselves. I haven't told you everything, you know. Would you like to hear the end of Sir Stephen's tale?

"Yes," I replied, thinking of the empty book beneath my jacket. I certainly could not read the end of the story there.

"The finale then," he said. "The Duchess of Burgundy came to the flooded tower near the end of Sir Stephen's life, no longer the powerful woman who'd held the allegory. Her strength and authority had diminished since the rise of the Hapsburgs, but she still dressed the part, wearing heavy robes colored like the skins of ripe plums and her hair was tangled with talismans. She looked more like a witch than an alchemist when she came to the flooded castle, and she sat with the old knight, Sir Stephen of Sorrows, holding both his hands. She was silent for so long, he wondered if she would reveal herself to be some specter, but when she spoke, her voice was thick with living care. She told him she was sorry for the poetry of the allegory. Sorry for the theater. She'd heard what had happened to his squire—to *Pieter*, for she knew the boy's name—and she was to blame for the Burning Armor. 'It was a foolish thing to make,' she said. 'Mere simulacra—layers of protection that did not protect, but I bring you a final gift.' She produced a letter from the pocket of her robe. 'The boy wrote to me years ago,' she told Sir Stephen, 'telling me of all the wonderful adventures he'd had at your side and how much he'd grown to love you. Pieter knew it was safe to say a thing like that to me. Listen here to his lines. And she read from the letter in the flooded tower, her voice echoing beautifully toward Glastonbury: *My knight has two hearts, one of iron to keep me safe and one of wax—so soft and warm. He presses me to that second heart and makes a mold of me. I know that I am there in him—a copy that will be loved even when I am gone.'* With that the Duchess folded the letter and leaned over the Burning Armor, kissing it on its Saint Andrew's cross. So you see, Kenton, even a part of the Duchess is there. All of them there in that box."

I turned to look at the crate again. It danced with shadows in the firelight, and I could indeed imagine all their ghosts crouched inside, attached to the Burning Armor, dragged by it through history. "Yes," I said. "You were right to buy it, and I thank you for the stories." He nodded in a gentleman's way, and because I knew he wanted nothing more from me, I clutched the empty book beneath my coat, shored myself against the cold and made my way toward the foyer and the snowy night. But I found I could not leave in that manner, knowing I might never encounter Lord Weymouth again, so I turned back and saw that he'd slouched in his chair, believing our scene complete. "Thomas," I said, "I want you to know that there was never a problem between us—even when we argued, even when I left you, it was all part of the good."

He attempted a smile, an air of levity, but could not raise himself from the chair. "We walked together didn't we, Kenton? For as long as two men could."

I don't remember leaving Longleat that night— returning to my carriage, traveling down busy streets of Christmas Eve revelers and finally recovering my wife. I must have done these things—yet it seems to me, in fact, I walked through a forest of long ago with the sun warming my skin, making me feel as if I were made of wonderful fire, a tilted cross carved upon the plating at my chest. I could hear singing. And yes, I was surprised to realize it issued from my very own astonished throat.

Beneath Us

FOR THE BETTER PART OF AN HOUR, I stood at the locked and painted gate of an unmarked graveyard, watching spotted hens and ducks of some ancient variety pick their way between fallen headstones. I'd slipped half inside a dream, charmed by the birds. They were black-eyed and mute, moving gently across the grass, sometimes grouping in the shade of a worn monument or at the perimeter of the fence.

Children had thrown clods of dirt at me earlier in the day for trespassing in what I believed to be a graveyard but turned out to be their mother's washing yard. I wanted to explain that I was an official, an emissary of the Queen, yet they were so angry and chiding, I could not speak. They believed perhaps I was the embodiment of some cruel woman they'd heard about in a fairy tale. My book and my dark dress, the creases around my mouth and eyes—all of this betrayed me. When had I become such a distasteful creature? Over what line had I stepped?

It was pleasant to simply take leisure with the ducks and hens, where I knew I would not be attacked. Apparently, this yard had been turned into an aviary years ago by some urban peasant, and I thought the dead should like to watch the comings and goings of animals, as I myself have often preferred the lower beasts to their supposedly evolved counterparts.

It is the will of the Metropolitan Gardens Association, my new employer, that all such consecrated grounds should be located, labeled, and preserved. Mrs. Octavia Hill, head of the board and fierce proponent of urban renewal, imagines these yards transformed into what she calls "outdoor sitting rooms," and the notion conjures curious pictures: a sofa of dewy lichen, a hearth that burns with untended violets. The difficultly is that the yards themselves have floated free from the churches and institutions to which they were once tethered; fires and the shifting tides of urbanization have razed those structures, yet the graves remain.

Before my deployment, Mrs. Hill, with the high and regal voice of a clarion, provided a collection of cautionary tales—hidden graveyards destroyed by property-hungry industrialists during the boom. Carbolic acid was used in many cases to dissolve the bones so no record of exhumation remained. "We must mark these grounds," she said. "Save the dead and save ourselves, Miriam. And it's women like you—childless and without other occupation who shall lead the way. You will become mother to our ancestors and therefore mother to us all."

And so I persist in my survey, mothering and dreaming, carrying the accordion-style grid map provided to me by the board and labeling it carefully as I have been hired to do. And I *am* thankful. Mrs. Hill is correct; women like me—nearly forty and without husband or station—are rarely allowed such new beginnings.

20 August

THE HEAT WAS LIKE A CEILING on Staining Street, and I struggled to remain upright. My newfound friend, Alain de la Tour, did not fair as well. He collapsed dramatically in the shade of a poplar tree, pale and dripping in his fashionable suit. Hand at his chest, he moaned comically, "Miriam. Oh, Miriam." He suffered from palpitations, and I told him that if he could not keep up with a rheumatic woman, he was clearly not taking enough morning exercise. He waved a porcelain hand, telling me the French did not exercise as the English. It was crass to even mention such a thing. "And you, my dear, are not as rheumatic as you seem to think."

I'd made his acquaintance at one of the new coffee palaces that have sprung up in the city's finer neighborhoods—glowing bargelike buildings full of girls in hats who believe they are made beautiful by lantern light. M. de la Tour approached my table in all his threadbare regality, and after a brief introduction, explained that he had arrived in London to make himself known to society, believing it would bring him either fame or wealth. Despite my wish to hurriedly dismiss him, I found that he possessed a magnetism—not animal but mineral, glittering like a sulfide extracted from the earth. A pyrite, lovely despite the fact that it played at being gold. He admired my map, asking if I were planning an invasion of some kind. When I explained my appointment at the Gardens Association, his polished eyes widened. My dress, he said, was not unlike Ruskin's storm cloud—a wind of darkness and my hair was a fall of ashes. Even at a distance I had appeared macabre.

"Is that flattery or insult?" I asked.

He ignored my question, sitting at my table without invitation and nearly spilling my demitasse. "I would like to take you to a party—a celebration of Regent's day," he said. "I am in need of a lady, and you are clearly in need of cheer."

I laughed politely. I had not attended a party since I was quite young and did not intend to take up the habit again. Even as I refused, I found myself wishing I was the kind of woman who *could* go to a party—not an actual English gala of course—which would certainly be of the same dull breed I remembered. No, I would have liked to attend the party the young man was imagining. Society as conjured by Alain de la Tour. I studied his poorly cut hair and provincial nose, features that seemed to indicate a lonely but hopeful mind, and I wondered what sort of place he'd come from. Certainly not a city. Alain only pretended at sophistication. A small village was more like it; something near the water with stony beaches.

*

I COVERED MY MOUTH AND NOSE with my shawl to prevent the smell of the nearby meat packing house from making me ill. Alain had tied a red silk handkerchief over his face and looked like a petite outlaw of the American West. As we walked, I related a story I'd been told during an interview with the abbess of St. Benet Sherehog. A gravedigger and his young apprentice had recently expired from bad air after climbing into an open pit grave of the sort still used in some of the country yards. "Bodies are wrapped in rugs or cloth," I said, "and with little ceremony they are dropped into the pit, jumbled together and sprinkled with lime until the space is full. Terrible gases are released from the corpses—what the diggers call 'poisonous air'." Alain reacted with picturesque disgust, asking why the diggers had gone down into the grave to begin with.

"To steal, most likely," I said. "People will brave poison for money these days. And it is exactly such mistreatment of the dead that I am working to prevent."

He swore an oath and said that in his country, the dead were respected. Cities were built to hold them—rows of grandiloquent tombs that verged on the Egyptian. "There are fog-laden boulevards" he continued, "and reflecting pools. Music is played and tragic tableaux enacted on stages by youths dressed in crepe." I had seen sketches of French cemeteries, of course, and knew they were similar to our English yards. Père-Lachaise was lovely but in a completely natural way. I was pleased though to hear Alain tell his stories. The right sort of lie, I found, could serve better than the truth.

The abbess of St. Benet Sherehog who'd directed me to Staining Street said she believed there had once been a church in the area attached to a burial yard. The church had burned (as did many of the churches) in the great fire of 1701, leaving the yard and its few monuments adrift. Houses had grown up around the yard, perhaps even over the top of it, though I hoped that was not the case.

I was admitted to the home of Mrs. Rayner Beloc, a quiet widow who, according to the knotted appearance of her hands, had lived a life of work. I left Alain on the street knowing that his extravagant nature might disturb her. Mrs. Beloc told me she'd lived in the same rooms for nearly fifty years and took her time before indicating that she was familiar with the burial yard I spoke of. In the heat of her cramped, spare parlor, she served cups of steaming Darjeeling, and we sat chatting near a soot-streaked window until finally, after she'd reminisced at some length about her husband who'd worked at the meatpacking plant, she pointed through the dirty portal, saying, "There is the yard you're looking for, Missus Isadore."

Below us, hemmed in by houses, was a square patch of ground growing not only tangled grass but tombstones.

"That's what's left of it, at least," said Mrs. Beloc. "I've known it was a churchyard for as long as I've lived in this house—anyone can see the white stones. How many of them do you count, Missus?" I was unsure of their number because of the poor visibility but thought I could make out eleven pale posts leaning in various directions.

Mrs. Beloc nodded. "That's what I used to think. But then I saw the twelfth, lying there at the northern end. Uprooted."

I leaned closer to the window and realized that Mrs. Beloc was correct. A twelfth headstone had fallen on its side in the late summer grass. "May we go down and visit the yard?" I asked.

"I've made attempts to do just that," Mrs. Beloc said. "Looks like it might be a peaceful place for a walk, doesn't it? When I was younger, I was want to do many such things. It would have been nice to walk there with my husband and read the names on those stones. But no matter how many doors I knocked upon, nor how many alleys I walked to their end, I could not find an entrance to that little yard. It's my belief there is no entrance, Missus. It can only be seen from windows. Perhaps it can only be seen from *my* window."

I put my tea cup carefully in its saucer, looking into Mrs. Beloc's deep-set eyes. "There must be some way, dear. It can't be entirely contained."

"My neighbors are kind hearts," she said. "All you need do is knock and they will show you there are no doors."

I did knock, and though I can't say I found all of Mrs. Beloc's neighbors to be the kindest of hearts, most did allow me into their homes long enough to discern that there was indeed no entrance to the small churchyard that the abbess of Saint Benet Sherehog had described to me.

"How can this be, Miriam?" Alain asked at the end of our search.

I shook my head. "Perhaps, in this case, the dead have decided to protect themselves."

29 August

TODAY, I VISITED the newly opened catacombs of St. Michael's cathedral on the arm of Alain de la Tour. He arrived at my rooms in a hired carriage with a charming yellow pansy in his lapel. We must have made an odd pair. I'm sure some of the women assumed I was his mother or a dowager aunt. At any rate, the crypt of St. Michaels, as advertised in the *Times*, had been refurbished and made into, of all things, a tearoom—and it was a truly astonishing space. A year before, the crypt was a festering tomb full of caskets, but it has been fastidiously cleaned and lit with gas lamps. Tea was served on lacquered tables and taffeta floated between the columns like aubergine clouds. Women of society promenaded through the catacombs as if in some quiet park on a sunless day, and I heard two of them remarking on the handsomeness of a medieval knight engraved upon the wall. Alain thought the whole thing ridiculous. "Have these people nothing better to do than wallow in their cult of death?" he whispered.

"It does seem a bit odd, doesn't it?" I replied, sipping my tea.

"More than odd," Alan said, dabbing sweat from his brow with a napkin. "If you wade too far into this black ocean, Miriam, you'll soon be swept away."

I told him I was not as morbid as he seemed to think. Most of my interests were quite normal: theater, novels, gardening and the like, which is how I'd become involved with the Metropolitan Gardens Association to begin with. I did, however, recall for him that as a child I'd witnessed a production of *Romeo and Juliet* in Regent's Park and had become rather fixated on the final set—Juliet's tomb, where the heroine lay in a magical state of both death and life. The players decorated the set beautifully with an ivy that nearly consumed the stage; twinkling lamps shone from between the leaves. How that place must have smelled to Romeo—not of decay but of vertiginous life with a tincture of apothecarean poison. "I pretended that my girlhood room was the tomb of Juliet," I said, "and I waited there for Romeo—not to kiss me back to life as does the dull prince in *Sleeping Beauty*, but to kiss me deeper into death."

Alain finished his tea in one gulp, leaned across the table, and kissed me brightly on the cheek. A fierce blush overtook me and I glanced around the crypt to see if anyone were watching. "This does not disprove my theory that you're a strange one, by the way, Miriam," he said. "Deeper into death? Come now."

I cleared my throat. "As I said, I was young, and Shakespeare can be quite romantic."

Alain grinned. "Your Shakespeare, too, is dead."

"The rose of yore is but a name," I quoted, and we stood to leave that place and return to the street above.

Beneath Us

1 September

I'M AFRAID ALAIN AND I HAVE ARGUED. It would be more fitting for me to write about the burial yards I have visited since my last entry, but I cannot think of them. I can only turn our disagreement over like a problem, though no solution presents itself. We'd taken a small boat to a lake-bound island called Curston's Stand where I'd heard there might be a lost burial yard. I'd received a message from Octavia Hill, asking if I could please hurry my work along, as she wanted to present my findings to next month's meeting of the board. She needed statistics—unmarked yards in danger of dissolution. I replied carefully to her note, saying that the more yards I plotted on the map, the more seemed to present themselves to me. I feared that soon I would have made one black mark over all of London.

The sun shone through a dolorous ceiling of clouds, coloring the day in a minor key. Alain was distracted as he paddled. Several times his hand went to his chest, and a look of concern shaded his features. I asked whether he was having palpitations as he had on Staining Street, and this question seemed to irritate him. He claimed there was nothing wrong that some common rest wouldn't cure and reminded me that he'd stayed out late the night before—an event to celebrate Empire Days, which I'd refused to attend—and now once again, here he was prancing about in search of the dead. "Anyone would be tired with a schedule such as this, Miriam. Anyone."

"You don't need to raise your voice," I said flatly. "And you don't *need* to join me on these excursions, you know."

"I suppose I don't," was his terse response. Then after a pause, he said, "I'm sorry."

97

"For what?" I asked. "We've only spoken the truth."

"You are crying, Miriam," he said.

I touched my cheek and found it wet. Having no notion of my emotional state disturbed me. Had I really grown so disconnected? As a younger woman, I'd allowed myself release, but in later years I'd become embarrassed by such things, the way that people looked at me, and worked to make them disappear. Primitive cultures called such a thing, "losing one's soul." Was I now nothing more than a shell that dragged itself along, a body ready for the grave? I turned from Alain to study a line of black ducks swimming near the shifting trees on the far shore. In the end, we found no graves on Curston's Stand, only the remnants of a picnic and an animal in such a state of decomposition that we could no longer tell its kind.

"I must be honest with you, Miriam," Alain said, standing by our little boat, leaning on the oar. "I no longer want to come on these ventures with you. Please don't be hurt."

I folded my hands and said of course I understood. "Have you met someone new?" I asked. "At Empire Days?"

"I have met many people," he said.

"And you prefer them to me?"

He shook his head. "I prefer them to death."

7 September

GRAMERCY PARK: DAY DARK AND WINDBLOWN. Near the pond, children played a game of Who Killed Cock Robin, and fragments of their chant drifted to me: *Who saw him die? I, said the Fly. Who caught his blood? I, said the Fish.* I'd brought an umbrella in case of rain, but no storm presented itself.

A single column of smoke had risen from a public fire fit for a Guy Fawkes celebration, making the sun look pale, as if it had emerged from beneath the sea. I went to the park alone. Alain and I had not spoken for nearly a week. Twice, I'd almost written to him, wanting to say that I'd imagined a home in the country—rolling hills of heather with not a graveyard in sight. But the embarrassment was too much. Whoever had invented love and marriage was dead now, too, and I was glad for that.

The men from Oxford, three of them in coats and fluttering ties, greeted me cordially before handing me off to a student. I was, after all, not a scientist but a mapmaker from the Gardens Association, and my quiet participation in urban reform meant little to them. At a portable table, the student showed me the items excavated from the hill: a spearhead, a broken coin, and a few fragments of bone. The theory was that the hill had served as an ancient burial mound for high-ranking Roman soldiers, though the Oxford men were perplexed as to why the soldiers had been buried *inside* the perimeter of the Roman wall. "If this is truly what it appears," the student said, "there could be thousands of such undiscovered plots all over the city, ma'am. The souls of Romans, spread everywhere about." He chuckled. "I hope you're not the type to have nightmares."

I assured him I was not and wanted to tell him of my own research but decided against it. The boy looked rather susceptible to nightmares himself. Instead, I asked for a closer look at the excavation, and he led me to the channel cut into the hill—a kind of low hallway with wooden braces to hold back the dirt, then he, too, excused himself. I was momentarily alone with the Romans, and I stepped across the line of rope, slipping into the passage and lifting my skirts to avoid dragging them in the mud.

From the tunnel, the park and sky were no longer visible, and I put my face close to the wall to look for some yet undiscovered artifact. The blunt smell of the earth filled my nose, and I could see nothing but shining bits of black rock and debris. The coolness was pleasant, conjuring enclosures from childhood: a hollow tree, my mother's dressing room. But then I began to feel claustrophobic, as though I was trapped in the hill—entombed. Nearly panicking, my lungs straining for air, I slipped and fell against one of the wooden braces, and it was then that I heard a quiet echo, like music that seemed to rise from the dirt itself. At first, I told myself the sound must be reverberation from some distant bandstand in Gramercy Park, yet the music seemed to grow louder, drawing me closer to the wall. Was there singing too? I believed there was. And those voices soothed my nerves, helped my body to relax. The edges of my form began to dissolve in the darkness of the hill. How many times had I heard death named a dreamless condition, yet ensconced within the mound, I realized that perhaps the dead *do* dream. This might very well be the music of their reverie, and listening to it made me feel a citizen of some other country. I dropped the hem of my dress, lowering my body against the inner belly of the hill. I held the dirt. For a moment, forgetting Alain and the attentions he'd paid to me.

15 September

THE SONG IN THE HILL—I am beginning to think it was mere delirium. Perhaps lack of oxygen or some freshly opened subterranean gas fissure caused the hallucination, though I can still remember the tune carried by those voices—rising and falling like waves—and I hum it under my breath at times. After the events in Gramercy Park, I grew weak with sadness. Terse letters from Octavia Hill arrived daily asking about the status of my research, but I could not respond. I felt I'd lost Alain and at the same time had become separated from my project. I was neither a scientist from Oxford nor a mystic who could commune with the dead. What was the point of my searching out graveyards? What good would my findings do in the end? Perhaps Alain was right. I'd spent my whole life afraid of the living, and now, via Octavia Hill and her reform movement, I'd found a silly reason to further remove myself from that world.

But that melancholy curtain seems to have risen, and I am once again ready to perform my duties. I sent word to Ms. Hill that my research was nearly complete, though I confess that was partially a confabulation, as I am not sure when I could actually call the work finished. I affixed my Gardens Association badge to my shawl and took up my map this morning with new resolve—fortified too by the return of Alain. I'd cleverly sent word of my intention to travel to Cripplesgate for an investigation of a possible occurrence of bodysnatching at a hospital yard, and he returned with a succinct note: *Miriam, you are a complete fool if you think I would let you go there alone. Be ready at eleven.* I knew, of course, that he would insist on protecting me, though Alain is something of a dollish man, and I worry that he might, in fact, draw the wrong sort of attention.

*

THE HOSPITAL, CALLED ST. JOHN'S OF JERUSALEM, was a Byzantine affair, and I was happy we did not have to walk its halls. I could hear the pained moaning well enough from

101

its windows and pitied the penniless men and women who were forced to convalesce there. Alain kept watch near the carriage, fidgeting nervously in his auburn suit while I approached the ancient gate of the adjoining burial yard and attempted conversation with the gravedigger, a tall man with a sandy face who sat smoking a reed pipe on one of the larger stones. The rusted metal of the gate peeled away like tree bark beneath my fingers, and the digger took his own time answering my inquiries. He said the men who filched the yard weren't called bodysnatchers; they'd been dubbed Resurrection Men.

"Like Christ himself?" I asked, not without humor.

"Doctors must have somethin' to study upon, ma'am," he continued. "Fresh bodies are hard to come by these days. Sometimes, if they are not given readily, they must be taken. We never use stolen goods here at St. John's though. You can tell your ladies at the garden society that." And from this protestation, I realized that St. John's was quite likely mining its own fresh graves. The digger was not a digger at all but a Resurrection Man. He went on to tell me that sometimes these Resurrection Men were also interested in fully decomposed bodies that were no longer wearing their flesh. "These," he said, "are sold to country churches desperate for bones to fill their reliquaries. Imagine the jaw of some John Doe being touted as a vestige of John the Baptist—only nobody better ask about his gold tooth." He laughed, and I excused myself quickly thereafter, marking my map as I walked.

Our hired carriage carried us further into Cripplesgate, and I began to count the small cemeteries that could be seen from the street, stopping when I'd reached twenty. How could there be so many? The poor were prone to death, but also apparently prone to exhibiting that mortality. There seemed a graveyard on every block. And all the

102

while, Alain recounted the details of a party he'd attended thrown by a countess. Apparently cave-aged cheese had been served.

I happened to catch sight of what may have been a woman or a young boy standing at the fence of one narrow, desolate yard. The urchin's gender was obscure because the figure's hair had been tonsured as is often done in preparation for the receiving of some religious rite. More than that, the clothes were not clothes precisely, but what I can only describe as a colorless shroud. When the creature saw my face, it put its hands on the bars of the graveyard fence and watched intensely. I tapped on the carriage ceiling, indicating that the driver should stop. I refused to listen to Alain's complaints as I hurried across the street to the fence. The closer I came to the poor wretch, the more its gender seemed to dissolve until I was looking at nothing more than a mask with the semblance of features hovering above a fluttering drape. It was a human face, yes, but somehow like the lower animals, too. The creature had pressed its body against the railing and seemed to require my help. Perhaps it had been hurt and was searching for kindness. "My dear," I whispered to it. "My dear, shall I let you out of there? There must be a gate 'round the other side." But Alain was already at my back, pulling me. "Miriam, hurry. Don't be foolish. We're in Cripplesgate, for God's sake." He was looking at the creature behind the fence in horror. I found myself unable to glance back as he rushed me toward the carriage. I did not want to see how the poor thing would watch us go.

Inside the safety of our vehicle, Alain was unable to control the features of his normally composed and handsome face. His full set of teeth shown in his mouth. His eyes were half-sunk into his head, and I could see the shape of his skull beneath his skin. "What were you *thinking?*" he whispered, as the carriage bucked to a start.

"I wanted to see if that child needed my assistance," I replied.

"Child?" he said. "Miriam, that was not a child. It was a lunatic of some variety I have never encountered before. This is the last time. Truly the last. I'm finished."

I tried to take Alain's hand and felt his pulse clanging in his wrist. "I'm sorry, dear. Sorry for frightening you," I said.

"Aren't *you* ever frightened?" he asked, pulling away from me. "Don't you have that capacity?"

19 September

I INTENDED TO BEGIN MY SURVEY of the plague pits today, many of which remain unmarked and date far back into our city's history. It is possible to locate such pits by doing careful research and speaking with the locals of various unpleasant neighborhoods. Bones, buried quite near the surface, are often unearthed by some interested dog. The plague pits inhabit enormous tracts of land—famous examples being Black Ditch and the Pardoner's Yard. There is a deep history of such pits going back to the first iteration of the plague in 658 when the Saxons perished by the thousands. I knew Mrs. Hill would be pleased if I located a few of the pits because a plaque could be erected. Also, such a difficult endeavor might take my mind temporarily off Alain. He had not made contact after the events in Cripplesgate, and could I truly blame him?

In the end, I did not go out. I sat in my parlor with the drapes shut tight, and thought about the figure at the fence. Who had it been or what? I tried to sketch it on a piece of paper but ended up tearing a hole in the sheet. A theory, known as Animism, had been recently put forth by spiritualists who believed that objects possess their own kind of life and, hence, volition. I wondered if what we'd seen had not been a person at all, but some piece of the burial yard itself, stepping forth to investigate me, the investigator. Perhaps I was not mother of the dead, but mother of the yards—the grass and the stone, coffin wood and statuary. I tried to put the thought aside as foolishness. The graveyards were not my children, and I was not their surrogate. What would Alain make of such considerations?

5 October

THIS EVENING I WITNESSED a torchlit night funeral of the sort still customary for suicides. Very few parishioners were in attendance. I did not go to the grave of the girl (for it was a girl who had taken her life), but rather sat on a marble bench and watched the procession. Her coffin came on a humble haymaker's cart decked with dyed ostrich plumes. A man played a dirge on a flute and another carried a portrait draped in black muslin. The face in the painting, presumably the girl's, was surprisingly like the face of the urchin I'd seen in Cripplesgate. It was a poorly executed likeness, an oversimplification of features done in oil, and yet it seemed to reach out to me—yet another object possessed with life. Animism again? I considered what it meant that suicides must be buried under cover of night, such a thing seemed foolish and cruel. Lines of poetry I'd memorized in childhood returned: *When he shall die, take him and cut him out in little stars. And he will make the face of Heaven so fine that all the world will be in love with night and pay no worship to the garish sun.* And what were the stars but bright gas and rock—monuments dangling from the firmament? I raised my head and tried to remember a prayer to say for the girl.

12 October

THIS EVENING I PUT ON my warmest cape and hood and ventured out to investigate one of the only private burial yards in the city. Such yards were outlawed early on in our history due to their tendency to spread bubonic plague. I'd come across information concerning the private yard by way of a Quaker woman who'd served as nanny to the daughter of the Earl of Dartmouth. The daughter had fallen on hard times and the Quaker had been dismissed from her position—the Earl blaming her for his daughter's misfortunes. I believe the Quaker felt vindicated in revealing the Earl's private yard to me, also whispering there was a rumor circulating that the ground was still accepting fresh bodies—a highly illegal act according to city ordinance.

I'd given up on the idea of asking permission to view the yard, as I was sure I'd be refused. Instead, I decided to visit the Earl of Dartmouth's property under the cover of night. It was only when I passed through his thankfully unlocked back gate that I realized there was some sort of celebration going on at the stone manor house which sat high on an ivied hill. Chinese lanterns spilled red light from the back veranda, and the chatter of guests came to me on the cold evening breeze. I did not concern myself with the social event, as my business was with the burial site, which appeared to be an ample distance from the party so that no one would notice or bother my investigation.

The small gated yard contained a sepulcher braced by an iron latticework and topped with a weather-stained angel. Two funerary urns sat on either side of the narrow door. There were no markers or plaques, only the bone-white house and its silent seraphim. I took out my map and pencil, making careful note of the yard's distance from Dartmouth manor, and it was then that I heard the sound—the faint and glittering series of chords, rising and falling, not like an ocean this time, but a secret pond in far-off woods. The music came not from the party but from the earth. I did not trust my ears. Could it be that I had not imagined the song of the dead in Gramercy Park? Once again I found my edges dissolving, and I lowered my body toward the earth.

I could not help myself from forcing my fingers into the dirt, pulling back first the layer of grass and then the soil, finally digging with both hands until, not more than a few feet beneath the surface, I came into contact with the lid of a box. It was a decorative piece—the sort of container a dowry is often kept in. Bright tulips had been painted on the lid, and it had clearly not been made for burial, but to sit proudly on some girl's shelf. As I pulled the box from the earth, the music intensified and grew more beauti-ful—full of longing. Without thinking I unfastened the latch, opening the box and throwing back the lid. There, a small body lay in a partial state of decomposition, the whole of it resting on a silver hand-stitched pillow. The singing—which had once again enfolded me inside its dream—told me that the little fellow was not restful, had not been respected. And just as I was about to close the lid and take the poor dear with me to find some minister who might properly inter him, I heard voices from the veranda, a cheerful laughter that floated down the hill. The voices of a man and a woman eclipsed the song of the dead child, growing louder and louder until the pair was standing at the gate to the private yard. It was Alain in a dapper suit and a young girl wearing a bow in her hair. What horror did I feel in seeing him? I was still half-dissolved by the music, my hair hanging down. My hands were covered in soil, my dress streaked in grass. When the girl saw what I had pulled from the earth, she put her small hand to her mouth, forcing her fingers tight against her lips and began backing away, eyes shining with terror until she broke into a run. And Alain was left staring through the bars of the fence. Face as white as ivory. He was statue. No, a child's plaything.

"You have to help," I said, gesturing at the dowry box. "This body needs us."

He held his hand to his chest, sinking slowly against the gate, eyes of stone, flesh of stone. For him, I was not a woman haunted by spirits of the yard; I was the thing that haunts—that which lingers along winding paths and in the shadows of monuments. I could not bear for him to see me like that. I wanted life, yet death wanted me more. I gathered the box and lid into my arms and hurried from the yard, leaving Alain forever this time.

*

I SIT IN MY PARLOR, the dowry box near my chair. I've gone through the *Times* twice searching for listings of infant mortality. There is nothing. No record of the dear's existence. It is difficult to concentrate. I can hear the yards—from Clerkenwell to Cripplesgate—a longing body made of loving sound. Victoria and her London are but a brittle boat of dreams floating on that dark, luxurious ocean. I lay my head against one velvet wing of my chair. I feel myself diving beneath the cold waves—so perfectly submerged. Fantastically alive.

This New and Poisonous Air

SHE BEGAN TO WAIT in the snow-swept square, the same place where village sheep pastured during summer months, and she thought she could smell the memory of them—damp wool and grassy dung. She tried hard not to make a game of pretending to *be* a sheep, knowing that would only make her look more like a child. She wore a piece of red fabric tied at her throat, having heard it was a sign. The men took the older girls who did this, gave them work. Following example, she lowered her eyes, glanced up again—a ship signaling. Death had swept out of the cities on the backs of rats and fleas. First came the rash, then the cough, an unseen guest knocking. Finally, a spread of boils. The body became a cauldron set upon a fire. Some said the arrival of the death would be signaled by a riderless horse, gaunt and gray, that would wander into the square and eat from dead winter grass. Others thought a voice would issue from the ground—listing the names of those set to die.

In the end though, cloaked riders had come and told them to prepare. The riders remained mounted, wearing leather masks that covered their mouths and noses, making it look like they had muzzles. The King's Dogs, she called them to herself. And the Dogs spoke roughly, saying the village would sicken, they'd fill all their graves and hurt for more. "Dig plenty of holes while you're still healthy," said one of the Dogs. "And don't any of you go accepting travelers into your homes. Tell them all to move along. People who come on the roads carry boils."

Soon enough Illinca's father and his men, known as the Irontooths for their strength, were busy moving bones from graves to the charnel house so there'd be more room to bury the plague dead and hopefully the disease itself as the Dogs had prescribed. While they worked, Illinca idled. The charnel house cut a thin shadow over the yard where she played. Sometimes she pretended to be Mother—all home and prayer, the logic of folded linens. Other times, she was Father, putting her back into digging ragged holes while talking of ghosts. She liked looking at the artifacts piled in the charnel alongside the exhumed bones—a sharpened silver tooth, the swollen binding of a forgotten Psalter, clay dolls with painted eyes, ever-open to ward off things that would steal from the dead. There was a skullcap, still neatly folded after a hundred years, and a porcelain arm that rose from a pile of debris, fingers stiff and accusatory. Her father called this the bric-a-brac of the underworld.

The Irontooths numbered eleven in all, and there was music to their digging—the muffled thud of shovel heads striking the ground and the hush of dirt falling from the blades. Sometimes one of them would pause and say, "I know this one's people. Let me be the one to roust him." And then he would jump into the grave and collect the bones, holding a ribcage gingerly like a muddy trap in which some animal was still alive. The men were kind to Illinca, their little audience, and brought her creatures carved from wood—elephants and monkeys and stranger things (monsters really) with two beaked heads and tusks protruding from their stomachs. One carved her what appeared to be a man who was trapped inside a wheel, hands and arms fused to the wooden circle. The man was naked but for his body hair, and his face was that of a grinning demon. She accepted these gifts and put them in her skirt pockets, pretending to be pleased. Her father's partner, Frenir, said, "Soon you'll have yourself a whole ark, Illinca. You'll float away from all this and be saved, won't you?" She imagined standing on the deck of a creaking ship, waving to her parents and her village, then turning to realize she was all alone with her wooden bestiary that had somehow grown to full size and stood unsteadily on matchstick legs, watching her with the dark holes they used for eyes. And when she turned to look toward home again, she saw nothing but a wooden sky upon a wooden sea.

*

Her mother fell sick along with so many others.

Illinca was playing on the road when she heard the soles of her mother's shoes scrape against the porch, then watched her step away from the house, moving in quick jerks. Illinca steadied herself for a lashing, but none came. Her mother only stared—face red, her blouse opened indecently. A rash, like the tail of a comet ran between her breasts.

"Mamma?" Illinca said.

"Have you said your prayers?" her mother asked.

"I have."

"Have you said all your prayers, my darling?" she repeated.

Her father dug the grave himself. By then so many were already gone that the cemetery was beginning to boil over—the King's Dogs had been right on that account. But her father found a special place for his wife, putting her deeper than the other bodies and tamping the soil. For a long time then, he sat cross-legged on her grave, holding his shovel in his lap. He talked to his dead wife, said things Illinca was too far away to hear. She stood near the charnel house and saw only that his lips were moving, like a fish pulled from the river.

After her mother was gone, Illinca's father wouldn't look her in the face, and an old neighbor agreed to take her in as his servant. He called her Anna, his dead wife's name. He was sick, not from the plague but from the infirmities of age. She was to bring trays to his bedside, read to him from the Bible, and brush his hair before he went to sleep. He often touched her arm while she brushed, remarking on the softness of her skin and saying, "Slower now, Anna. My scalp is so tender." He died one evening while she watched, holding his hands against his mouth as if embarrassed by the final words that might slip out. Her father told no more stories of ghosts and began carrying a woodcut in his pocket showing the Virgin with the infant Christ standing on her knee. The child was crudely etched, looking more like a grim man than a baby, two fingers of the same length raised in a sign of peace. Her father wept over his dinner and once threw his wooden bowl against the wall with such force it left a mark that Illinca could not rub clean. A week later, he told her he was leaving the village for a digging job with the Irontooths. "I'll be back before month's end," he said. "I'm sorry to go, but the money will be good. Many gravers have fallen into their own yards."

"But you'll be a traveler," Illinca said. "Travelers spread disease."

Her father could not find it in himself to respond, and the Irontooths waved from the backs of their tall horses. Illinca's skirt pockets bulged with her collection of carved animals, and just as she feared, she was left alone with them feeling too young and foolish to guess the next step.

*

WHEN HEINRICH ADLE ARRIVED in the square, two months had passed since her father's leaving, and Illinca was becoming frightened. She tried her best to seem cheerful, sticking out her little tongue to catch snowflakes, holding the red fabric against her throat so the wind did not whip it away. She understood now that the fabric was a sign, though of what, she didn't know. Perhaps it meant the wearer was free from disease, free to be a wife. But Illinca was not taken like the other girls. When she realized a man was actually watching her, she composed herself, trying to look sweet, but when she saw exactly *who* was watching, she nearly laughed. This man wore the strangest clothes—a cloak lined with silk the color of new pumpkins, a soft hat that fell over one eye, and a heavy-looking talisman around his neck—a brass cross with a hole in its center. She knew he was not from their village, and had only a moment to wonder how a traveler had gotten in. Maybe people were too sick to bar the way.

Heinrich Adle stooped to examine Illinca, and she saw that his face was oddly cleaved—chin, lower lip and forehead all dented with the same vertical line, as if he'd been hit with an ax. He looked something like a book held open to a page. "Are you eating snow because you're hungry?" he asked.

She tried for charm. "Snowflakes don't satisfy, sir."

"Then we must find something that will," he said, mustache rising above crooked teeth.

"What would that be?" she asked, feeling that at any moment she might learn the secret of the red fabric.

"Satisfaction is variable," he said. "Finding the proper source is an art. Luckily, you have met satisfaction's sculptor." He extended his hand and she took it, finding his skin warm and his nails clean. "I am Heinrich Adle from Alland."

"Illinca," she said, forgetting to report her surname because she was trying to remember if she'd heard of Alland. She was fairly sure she hadn't and wondered if it was a made-up place, and this man was indeed as mad as he looked.

"And how many years have you seen, Illinca?"

"Ten," she replied, refusing to drop her gaze from his. "Or at least that is my estimation. How many have you seen, sir?"

"An unfortunate number," he said. "I wish that it were ten." He paused, as if trying to remember an important detail. "You know you are too young to be standing in the square. Have you parents?"

"Gone," she said. "The death took Mother, and my father is digging graves in other villages with his men, the Irontooths. Gone two months." She touched her red scarf. "I'm learning to make do for myself."

Heinrich Adle let out a quick laugh. "Is that so?"

Illinca wasn't pleased—the other girls never got laughed at. If anything, they were approached with a kind of reverence.

"Where did you say these Irontooths are?"

"Another village," she said, not wanting to show her full ignorance of the details, "to the south."

"Of course," he said. "I should have remembered that I'd heard talk of their name. Listen, my dear, I'm about to leave this place, as my job is done, but if you'll come along, I think we might just be able to find these Irontooths of yours. You could be with your father and not forced to stand out in this cold. What say you, little Illinca?"

She felt her insides vibrate with tones of pure joy. She missed her father terribly, and in recent weeks, she'd woken time and again from a dream in which he never returned. Months passed, then years, and she grew older in their thatched cottage, hair turning white, nose and ears distending, until one day she finally gave up on waiting and slumped to the floor.

"You'll not harm me?" she asked.

"Harm you?" Herr Adle replied. "Why in the world would I do something like that?"

She half-closed her eyes because she thought it made her look intelligent. "What motive do you have to take me on a journey?"

Herr Adle sighed. "I am in need of a girl, that's all I'll say at present, my dear. There's an element of theater to my trade. Remove the red scarf and come with me, if you will. Otherwise, remain." When he turned to leave, Illinca realized this was not a time for logic. Even her mother, who'd been logical about everything outside of God, would have agreed. If Father would not return, it was time to set out after him. Herr Adle's carriage was hidden in the shadowed alleyway behind the bakery that had been closed for weeks because the man and wife who'd owned the shop had succumbed. The carriage was made of polished wood and had real glass windows, something Illinca had never seen. There was a driver, wrapped in a thick blanket, who appeared to be in a deep sleep. Heinrich Adle tapped the man's knee. "Be quick," he said. "And don't light the lamps. We needn't make a scene on our way out."

She marveled at the warmth as she stepped into the woody sweetness of the carriage and sat on a pillowed bench across from Herr Adle who'd crossed his legs and removed his formless hat, patting it like some animal. "Are you a nobleman, sir?" she asked.

"I'm afraid not, dear."

"But you have such wealth."

He paused, the crease in his face looking ever more like the center of an open book. "I suppose you could say I'm a *visitor* to noblemen," he said.

Illinca was fairly sure that was not the name of an actual trade, but then again she didn't know everything about the world. In fact, her parents hadn't bothered to tell her that much at all. Her mother spoke of the mysteries of God and her father talked of old stories, but as for the actual world and how it worked, they'd said little, most likely because they knew little themselves. Illinca tried to think what to say next, still attempting to deduce what Herr Adle wanted from her. Obviously it was something that a red scarf could provide, otherwise he would not have chosen her. She remembered a thing she'd seen her father do to her mother once. "Are you going to kiss my breasts and hair?"

Herr Adle's yellowish eyes grew slightly wider. "My dear," he said. "Your breasts—as you call them—well—you have less of a those than I do. And your hair, it doesn't appear you've cleaned that in weeks."

Illinca felt her cheeks redden and willed them not to betray her childishness. "Will you kiss it if I wash?" she said.

"No," Herr Adle replied. "I don't think that will be necessary, Illinca. And at any rate, I shouldn't think your father would be pleased."

They journeyed for what felt like hours, and Illinca was fascinated by the idea that she had become a traveler. She was now an illegal spreader of the Mortality along with Herr Adle, but what better thing to be now that death was everything? The countryside was dark—perhaps the moon had fled to another place like so many wealthy citizens. Herr Adle closed his eyes and seemed to sleep while Illinca watched the landscape. She'd never seen these forests and lakes and thought that at any moment she might catch a glimpse of her father and the Irontooths, and she wondered if she'd run to him or pretend she'd turned into a lady who rode in polished carriages and could not be bothered with the likes of gravers. She'd only carry on the charade for a few minutes, of course, to punish him for leaving her for so long. But she did not see her father or any of his men, and when the carriage hit a road-hole, it bounced so violently that Herr Adle awoke, grabbing his hat and stuffing his hands inside for warmth, then slowly realizing that Illinca was watching him. "What is that you keep in your skirt pockets?" he said.

She reached into her still bulging pockets and produced two handfuls of wooden monsters which Herr Adle looked at carefully. "The Irontooths made them for me," she said.

From the pile, he selected the little man bound inside a wheel, hairy body stiff, face contorted in fear and rage. "This one is quite powerful. How do you interpret it?"

She shrugged. "It doesn't have a meaning, as far as I know. It's meant as a toy, though I'm too old for that sort of thing."

He handed the little man back to her. "Keep hold of these treasures, my dear. It's not every day that I see creatures quite so interesting."

She settled back against the cushioned seat, pleased to have shown him something new, and soon the carriage arrived at a fine stone house bordered on either side by thickets of trees and brake ferns. A candle hovered in the front window, illuminating the long face of a maid who stooped to watch Herr Adle and Illinca emerge. "Is this your house?" Illinca asked, drawing the collar of her ragged dress higher to protect herself from the cold night wind.

"If only," Herr Adle said. "I told you, I believe, that I am a visitor by trade. This is the home of a friend of mine who's abroad and has been kind enough to invite us to lodge here in his absence. Now, you need to curb your inquisition once we get inside, my girl. You may betray our secrets."

"What secrets do we have?" she said.

He patted her head. "Quite a few, I'd say."

Illinca was still confused but composed herself. She had to save her questions for important things. "Will we find my father in the morning?"

"Perhaps," Herr Adle said, pausing to consider. "But you must prepare yourself that we won't find him until the next day or the day after that. At any rate, soon, dear, very soon, and in the meantime, I shall keep you fed and happy."

*

HE DID NOT LIE. The two were served roast lamb and fennel in a room with pressed metal walls that reminded Illinca of being inside a large oven. Over the course of the dinner, Herr Adle talked a great deal, telling Illinca about the plague towns he'd seen. "Absolutely dripping with pestilence," he said, gesturing with his silver fork. "I saw a woman who died on laundry day, hung herself over the line between the linens, if you believe it. And I saw a man with half his head half-rotted off, still hammering at a piece of wood, as if *work* was that important."

"Why haven't you taken sick?" she said.

He paused, chewing his lamb. "I could ask the same of you, couldn't I, my little dear? Perhaps we're both angels, descended to view this horror but remain untouched."

"You don't need to talk to me like that," she said.

Herr Adle raised his black eyebrows, "Well then, most likely our humors are somehow suited to this new and poisonous air."

Illinca pushed at her food on the bone-colored plate, her stomach feeling more full than it had in years. "May I ask another question, Herr Adle?"

He wiped his mouth, then tossed the napkin aside. "If you must. But please don't let the maids hear. They really are such cunts at this house."

"What's cunt?"

"A person of no manners," he replied.

She committed this word to memory and then said, "You don't think something's happened to my father, do you?"

"I thought the Irontooths were strong men, Illinca."

"Oh, they are. I saw one of them bend a metal bar with his bare hands once, and another can chop down a tree with only five blows of an axe."

"Then nothing has happened to them," he said, matter of fact. "Nothing at all."

She imagined she was turning the pages of Herr Adle's booklike face, searching for answers, but finding only a language she didn't understand. After dinner, he dropped to one knee and spoke quietly to her. "The maids will see you to your room," he said. "You need not speak to them or ask their names. They're going to provide you with a costume. Take it graciously and go to bed."

"A costume?" Illinca asked.

He plucked at his odd cloak with the pumpkin-colored lining. "I have mine and now you shall have yours. And one more thing, dear—in the night, it's important that you stay in your room. These large houses can be very dangerous when all the lights are put out. There are ghosts."

Illinca nodded silently. She knew of ghosts.

"You're not afraid, are you?" Herr Adle said.

She snapped her heels like a little soldier. "There's nothing to fear, sir."

He laughed, and then they both laughed together. Herr Adle left her then with the sour-faced servants who acted like she was something they'd found in the yard. She watched as he mounted the stairs and entered a door at the end of the landing, marking its place in case she needed him. The maids took her to a small bedroom and gave her three dresses—one made of pressed velvet with glass beads sewn around the neckline and the other two of cotton with white lace. They even provided a small valise in which to carry these articles, and at that point, Illinca couldn't help herself. She had to ask. "Whose things are these?"

The two maids paused, the one with darker features frowning at the lighter one. Finally, the darker said, "They belonged to the little Missus, didn't they now?"

"She doesn't need them still?" said Illinca. "I don't want to take her nice things."

"On no—she's in the ground," the lighter maid responded. "As far as I can count, she only needs one dress there."

Illinca felt a rush of sadness for the dead girl and wondered too if this had been her bedroom. She didn't ask the maids because she was fairly sure of the answer and had no interest in terrible dreams. That night, she woke to the sound of the wind creaking the great house like a ship, and she sat up in bed to see that her old rag dress was still on the chair where the maids had hastily tossed it, but the wooden creatures had spilled from the pockets and onto the floor. Two of them had broken. One of the heads had snapped off the two-headed bird, and the goat-faced cat had lost its fragile horns. Illinca knelt on the floor and held both of them for a while, trying hard not to cry there in the dark, thinking of the Irontooths and her father. She wrapped all of the animals in her old dress, which from now on, would simply act as a cushion for her treasures, hopefully providing the animals some needed protection. She'd hate to break any more because, as Herr Adle said, they were objects of interest in a world that was emptying of such things. When she turned to get back into bed, she thought better of it. She needed to find Herr Adle and ask him to name a definite day they would find her father. She'd been foolish to come this far without some notion of schedule, and she hated herself for a moment for being so imprudent and girlish. If they didn't find him, she would request that she be returned to her village so she could wait in the cottage. She wondered, just for a moment, if Herr Adle would refuse this request, but as of yet, he'd been nothing but kind, so she put the idea away.

Illinca crept along the black hall, not afraid of ghosts or devils but of the maids—Dark and Light—who'd probably pinch her if they found her and tell her more cruel things about their dead Missus. She reached the oaken door at the end of the landing, the one through which she'd seen Herr Adle disappear earlier and knocked softly enough, making sure she'd wake no one else. A rustling came from within, and finally the door opened to show a crack of face, but the man who looked out at her was not Herr Adle. This person had straw-colored hair and a mole on his chin. "What is it?" he asked.

"Is Herr Adle in the room?" Illinca said.

The straw-haired man looked at her. "Who?"

"Herr Heinrich Adle, the visitor," she said. "This is his room."

The man seemed angry now. "I can assure you that this is no one's room but mine. Are you one of the maid's children?"

She stepped back. Her feet were bare and the floor suddenly felt very cold. The man opened the door wider to peer at her, and in the shadows beyond him, Illinca saw Herr Adle's pumpkin-colored cloak hanging from one bed post. "Are you not his friend?" she whispered, "the one who invited us to stay? Is that not his cape?"

The man's eyes narrowed as if what she'd said was completely mad. "If you're through with your games, little girl," he said. "I'd like to return to my sleep." He slammed the door, and she refused to jump at the frightening loudness of the sound. Illinca walked the halls, fearing that Herr Adle had abandoned her, an idea that made no sense. Why could he play such a cruel joke? At a time of such uncertainty, there would be no advantage to duping a child. The maids seemed to know him and he'd certainly entered that room only a few hours before. His pumpkin cloak even hung on the post. So what had happened to put things so out of joint? She looked for clues in the house, but found only a large wooden clock in a room full of dusty books, some of which were larger than even her mother's Bible. The clock had eyes painted on its face, two staring orbs, and in the darkness they were first her mother's soft eyes and then her father's. She put her arms around the big clock and held it, feeling it tick against her narrow chest, like her own heart beating.

Illinca remembered a story her father had told her about a man who could change his shape at will, becoming an animal and then a man again. "He was a kind of devil, to be sure," her father said. "He couldn't live like a civilized person because he was always turning into a bird or a wolf or a bat and fleeing into the countryside, and when he turned back into a man, he never looked the same as the man he'd been before." She wondered if Herr Adle was a thing like that, a changing demon, though part of her knew better. Only darkness and her own fear made her think such things. If Herr Adle changed, he did so in nature, not in form.

When the dark maid woke her at dawn, Illinca asked if Herr Adle had abandoned her. The maid crossed her eyes and stuck out her tongue. "Of course not, stupid child. If he left you here for me to wipe your ass, I'd go after him myself and wring his neck. The last thing we need is another brat bawling about her cough and rash." She found Herr Adle seated at the table in the pressed metal room, eating a breakfast of boiled eggs and bread. When he saw Illinca in her new dress, he acted like she was the daughter of the king, bowing to her and helping her into her own chair. She watched him carefully, not asking about the man she'd seen the night before. Instead, she checked for any trace of blond in his dark hair or the shadow of a dissolving mole.

*

THAT DAY, THE CARRIAGE WAS HALTED on the road near a marsh, and when Illinca saw who'd stopped them, she felt like a hand was at her throat. The King's Dogs, wheezing through their leather muzzles, ordered the carriage driver to dismount and open the door, hurrying the poor man along with their cudgels. They could certainly see Herr Adle and Illinca plainly enough through the glass, just as she could see them, and once the door was opened, one of the Dogs, who had a yellow crust built over his left eye said, "No one is to be on this road."

Herr Adle leaned against the brass handle of the carriage door and said, "I'm taking my daughter to her mother in the south. We understand the restrictions, but I'm afraid if I do not get her there soon, they'll never see each other again."

The Dog glanced back at the other riders who were having a conversation of their own and then examined Illinca with his good eye. She tried to smile, which is what she thought a daughter of nobility would do. "You both should be imprisoned," the Dog said.

"The open countryside has become prison enough for us all," Herr Adle said with poetic air, then he gave a mild cough, and the Dog drew back, blinking in surprise.

Illinca started coughing too, as hard as she knew how, putting her hand over her mouth and attempting to appear frightened by the force of her expectorations. The Dog withdrew, circling his horse with the others. "Be certain not to stop along the way, imbeciles," he said. "The Mortality spreads, you know?"

"I'm well aware," said Herr Adle, waving a hand dramatically, as if to draw air to his lungs.

The carriage door closed, sealing Herr Adle and Illinca in shadows of mutual understanding. "Is that why you need me?" she whispered. "To play a fake daughter for you?"

"Among other things, dear. Your services are not limited, but certainly men with daughters in tow are a more sympathetic lot," Herr Adle said. "Especially sick little daughters. Good work on that piece of dying, Illinca. Even without my coaching."

"What if we're stopped again?" she said.

He touched the top of her small hand, stroked its veinless surface. "Then we'll repeat the game of sickness. Hone our work, as good performers do."

"My father says those horsemen work for the king," she said.

Herr Adle sighed. "No one really works for the king anymore, dear. We're on our own."

"Not us though," she said. "We work together."

He patted her. "That's right, and don't worry, Illinca. You won't be harmed. I'll protect you. You have my bond." Then he coughed once more, even though they were all alone, and there was no one for whom to put on a sickness show. The beads on the dead girl's dress felt suddenly too tight against Illinca's throat. "I thought you were pretending that," she said.

He waved his floppy hat. "Merely the aftereffects of stage play. The world is right. Now take your nap."

But when Illinca closed her eyes, she saw only the red comet of a rash running between her mother's breasts, and now too she could hear its roar.

*

That night, instead of going to another fine home, they stayed in a broken-down inn, partially blackened from an old fire and run by a crude-looking woman who'd cut her gray hair short, probably due to a case of vermin. There was a small tavern room with a bar of pine wood, and the woman kept an oddly dressed doll next to her while she worked. She seemed to recognize Herr Adle, and when he and Illinca were in the midst of eating an awful dinner of pickled ham and a loaf of hard bread, the barmaid asked, "Didn't you have a different girl with you the last time you was here?"

Herr Adle stiffened. "Keep to your business."

The barmaid squinted at them both, and Illinca thought her small pink eyes were piggish. "Least my business is of a clean sort," the maid said.

"You have obviously not taken a night's repose in one of your stinking rooms if you labor under that delusion," Herr Adle replied, turning his back on the crone.

"Is it true?" Illinca whispered. "Did you travel with another girl before me?"

He nodded absently, gnawing on a bite of greasy meat.

"And *she* too played your daughter?"

"That's right, dear. But the Mortality took her some months ago." He raised the brass cross that hung around his neck and kissed the hole at its center. "I buried her in a pretty place beneath some willows." He coughed quietly into the back of his hand so the barmaid wouldn't hear.

"Did she give you the Mortality?" Illinca asked, wanting to put her hand to his forehead as her mother had once done for her, but as she had not been allowed to do for her mother.

"No one gives the Mortality to another," he said. "It simply *is*. The plague's in every element except fire, which won't tolerate it. At any rate, I am not diseased."

"But you have the cough."

"I have *a* cough. Not all afflictions of the throat are the black death."

Illinca watched the barmaid pace, cradling her doll and cooing to it. "What was the other girl's name?" Illinca said finally.

He looked pained to recall, the crease in his face growing deeper. "She didn't have a proper one, but I called her Petal because she was soft."

"Petal," she repeated, committing herself to remembering that name, so the girl who lay beneath the willows would not be entirely lost. Then quietly, she said, "And did this Petal have a father you promised to deliver her to?"

"Illinca," Herr Adle said sharply. "I mean what I say about taking you to find the Irontooths."

She pushed her plate away, not angry but full of new understanding. Herr Adle made use of girls to create cover for his own activities, his *visiting*. Whatever the lie he'd told Petal, she'd taken it with her to the place beneath the willow trees, and yet knowing this did not make Illinca hate Herr Adle or even fear him. In fact, she imagined Petal had been happy, much as she was happy now. If girls were necessary to Herr Adle's free movement about the country, then they were significant to him, even precious, in a way. Being necessary to someone was not unlike being loved.

After dinner, Herr Adle took her by the hand and led her to a room where a filthy mattress lay on the floor stuffed with damp straw. He slept next to her that night, very close, almost holding her, and she was glad to have him there. She awoke before dawn to starlight drizzling through the open window and found that the dusty blanket had been thrown back and Herr Adle was gone. Slipping out of bed, she cracked the door and peered into the hall. A few doors down, a man with red hair and skin blotches (not the black boils, at least) stood smoking a reed pipe and talking to another man who slouched like a drunkard. The man with blotches noticed her first and gestured. "There's the one he travels with," he said of Illinca.

She was frozen, unable to close the door or even slip back into her room.

"Maybe *she* might be of some use in his stead," said the drunken man.

The blotchy one laughed. "Tight fit, that one. But I suppose after a few rounds she'd loosen up."

"Or we could do some fancy knife-work," said the drunken man. "Age her a few years with artistry."

Illinca finally found the strength to close the door against their laughter and then sat with her back to the splintered wood. Her heart beat so hard against the door, she was afraid the men would hear it, and she could not say how she fell asleep again, reclining there, barring entrance to the room. In the morning, she roused herself, and once she realized no breakfast would be served, she gathered her things and went out to the black carriage, where Herr Adle sat bundled in his cloak. Only his eyes and the tip of his nose were visible, though, by his posture, she could tell his illness had worsened in the night. She reached into her folded skirt, feeling around for the right creature, and finally produced the one whose arms and legs were fused to the wooden wheel. She handed it to him and said, "For you."

He studied the thing with less than normal amusement.

"I found a meaning for it," she said. "It's not just a toy—it's like you. Always turning but unable to leave the wheel."

He half-smiled at the carving.

"Who were those men in the hall last night?" she said.

"Those?" he said, then coughed hoarsely. She had to wait for him to finish. "Those are the ones I see if no one better wants to employ me. I'm sorry if they scared you, dear."

"It's all right." Illinca clicked the heals of her shoes and said quietly, "Nothing to fear, sir. Nothing to fear at all."

*

They traveled on, sometimes sleeping in the carriage, sometimes in a convenient place they found. Illinca no longer asked about her father, instead centering her questions around the topic of Herr Adle's health. They made three more visits, two at fine houses and one in a place that was no more than a cave with several naturally formed rooms, as dank and unlivable as any Illinca had ever see. A gray-haired woman lived there with a tall man whose skin was white as cream. The old woman offered to let Illinca inhale some powders that she said would make the dead visible to her. "I don't need the dead," Illinca replied. "Not while I have Herr Adle."

"Your friend is sick," the old woman replied. "You'll surely need powder soon to see even him, little one."

"I'll soon need powder to see *everyone*," Illinca responded. Herr Adle would have laughed, but the cave woman did not.

"You know what your friend is, don't you?" she asked.

"A visitor," Illinca said, firmly. "We visit together."

Now the cave woman grinned. Illinca turned away. She knew, of course, what Herr Adle was. She'd even come upon him lying naked with one of their hosts. His eyes had been closed at the time, and he didn't know she'd seen. Certainly, she didn't need to hear a mad old woman provide a vulgar name for his work. It was what he *had* to do to survive.

She left the cave and found the white morning sky so big and full she thought it might crush her, and then when she saw Herr Adle lying on the side of the road like some discarded baggage, and she knew she *had* been crushed. Illinca ran to him and tried to remove the pumpkin cloak which he'd pulled over his face. "Don't touch," he said, which set off a fit of coughing. She hadn't seen her mother get so ill, as her father had kept the two of them separate, hoping to protect Illinca from the disease. "Where's the carriage?" she asked. The road outside the cave, as far as she could see, was empty.

"The old driver took it," Herr Adle whispered. "I couldn't pay him or fight him for it anymore." His legs were crumpled beneath him, bent oddly at the knee. Illinca looked back to the cave where the hag woman was with her powders and the pale man. There was no help to be found there. "Let me see what's happened," Illinca said, pulling at the cloak again, hard enough this time to force Herr Adle to release his grip. A black boil had appeared at the base of his neck, and the whole of it seemed to be pressing at his throat, as if a creature was trapped beneath the surface of his skin. The pressure made it hard for him to breathe, and Illinca forced herself to remain still and watchful as Herr Adle's very essence seemed to struggle for escape. She thought again about her father's story of the shape-changing demon. Whatever remained constant in such a creature, whatever ghost haunted its core, was what wanted out of Herr Adle now.

"How does it look?" he asked, pressing his square, clean fingers against the boil.

"We need to clean it," she said. "I can get some water. I think I saw a pond." But she wasn't sure that she'd *actually* seen a pond, or more correctly, she'd seen many ponds, but had there been one within walking distance of the cave? When Herr Adle looked at her, she saw that the possibility of a pond didn't matter. "Illinca, it can't be cleaned." He coughed again and this time pinkish liquid spilled from between his crooked teeth. She stooped to clean his mouth with the hem of her dress, but he pushed her away. "I shouldn't have brought you here," he said. "I was acting so selfishly. I'd never heard of the Irontooths. But you know that, don't you?"

She crouched. "Everyone's heard of the Irontooths. Stories of their strength precede them."

"I lied because I needed you to travel," he said.

"And you thought you'd be well," she said. "You thought *we'd* be well. We were angels, remember?"

"I was never that."

She sat down next to him in the cold dust of the road. "What did you do for Petal when she was sick?"

"Sang to her," he said.

Illinca tried to think of a song but realized all she knew were graver's chants, so instead she said, "I'll make a show for you instead. Something to look at." She fetched her folded rag dress from the dead girl's valise, took out all the wooden creatures and began placing them in a careful circle around Herr Adle's crumpled form. As she placed each, she gave it a name. "This is Candle Flame because of its eyes. And this one is Cunt because it has no proper manners. And here are Dark and Light, the devil maids. Here are Fat Cap and Reed Pipe. This is Knife Blade and Willow Tree."

The features of Herr Adle's face seemed finally at rest. "I know their names, dear," he said. "I know all of them."

After she'd finished putting out the monsters, Illinca sat for a while contemplating in silence, then asked, "Why do you think that no one took me from the square, Herr Adle—all the men only stared at me—was I too young?"

The booklike fold in his face had smoothed, growing almost nonexistent, as if an unseen pair of hands were stretching its covers. He took a long breath, then said, "No one is too young, Illinca. There are men who would have taken you."

"Then why?"

He wiped bile from his mouth with the back of his hand. "For the same reason you are not touched by the plague, I suppose—because the world has found some sympathy."

"That seems a dangerous thing to believe, Herr Adle," she said. He did not respond, and Illinca didn't force him. Instead she considered the circle of wooden beasts again—wondering if they'd somehow provided her protection, if the gravers had understood them not as toys but as talismans. She decided she would leave them on the road, just as they were and wondered what some other traveler would make of their configuration. What mystery would he imagine had been enacted here?

"If you're strong enough," she said, "we should walk. We need to find a house or barn where we can spend the night." Herr Adle's soft cheek lay against a stone, and he did not move. His eyes no longer searched for her, but instead seemed to silently ask what could be the point of traveling now that there were clearly no Irontooths to be found, no visiting to be done? Illinca drew tall in her new velvet dress. The point, she understood, was to do what was necessary—to move as a poison in a poisonous world. If they traveled far enough, maybe they'd find a part of the country where the air was kinder and Herr Adle could begin to recuperate. She would not let him die. Too many had died already. And if the pestilence had spread to all corners of their country? Illinca would find a bridge or perhaps a boat to ferry them. She understood there were solutions to problems like this and a real traveler would find a solution, so she took Herr Adle's cold hands and started to pull with all her strength, slowly at first, dragging him down the road behind.

Gardens of the Moon

No HORSE WOULD APPROACH the McCormick threshing machine once its steam engine had clattered to life and shot an antique column of coal smoke into the pale autumn sky. Bill had to put the skittish animals in the stable and pull the grain wagon into place himself, hoisting one shoulder against the leather harness and dragging the wagon to a spot beneath the thresher's tin arm. His new wife, Minarette, looking dollish in her city clothes, watched him work from behind the rippled glass of the farmhouse window, sipping coffee from a Chinese cup. The McCormick shook the ground as its flywheel quickened, and Bill fed sheaves of newly harvested wheat into the mouth, listening as the internal rakes and shakers cut grain heads from straw and then banged the seed from the chaff. When a river of golden wheat had begun to spill from the arm into the wagon, he mounted the engine that was attached to the thresher by train tongue and canvas belt and climbed through heavy smoke to reach the platform where the throttle provided some control over the leviathan.

Bill hurried the work, more concerned with the road than the harvest and keeping an eye on the strip of dirt that led to town, hoping to glimpse a rising trail of wagon dust. He anticipated a visitor, his boyhood friend Calvin Hascomb, come to say goodbye before heading off to divinity school in Toledo, but it was already late in the afternoon—the light had gone golden—and Bill was no longer sure that Cal would come. In that event, he told himself he would continue to work the thresher—this day and then the next, until harvest was done. Then he would help his father ready the farm for winter. This had been their pattern since he was ten years old. But when he pictured Cal departing without paying final respects, the sun beating down on his icy blond hair and clear eyes fixed on an invisible point in the horizon, Bill found he could barely lift another sheaf.

The McCormick bucked hard against its rotating belt, and Bill adjusted the throttle, reducing the flow of steam enough to temper the drive wheel. He wanted to kick the thing for requiring such attention. The newer, more urbane thresher, made by the J. I. Case Company, had broken down days ago, and Bill's father had cursed its modernity in Old World Dutch as he stalked off to the barn to pull the tarp off the old McCormick. Bill stood by the horse trough with his hands stuffed in the pockets of his trousers, one boot heel digging nervously at the dirt, and watched as the McCormick emerged from the dark hold of the barn, wagon wheels slowed by mud, spokes strung with woolly cobwebs. "That'll probably reap one of us before harvest is through," Bill called to his father. The old man ignored the comment, clenching his jaw and pushing the machine further into the light.

The thresher was the size of a grand piano turned on its side and painted crimson red, and over its hundred-odd years of service, it had developed a frightful personality and a talent for toying with any steam engine that powered it. The McCormick could grip the canvas rotating belt hard at times, causing the engine's flywheel to stick and squeal, building up an excess of high-pressured steam, then just as suddenly, it would release the belt so the engine would nearly burst. In this way, it had taken four of Bill's uncle's fingers during the harvest of 1902 when it had overheated the iron cylinder and finally blown the boiler, sending jets of hot steam and shrapnel in every direction and melting the very flesh of Uncle Dean's hand into something that looked like an overgrown cherry pit.

The incident occurred only three years after the flood had driven the Von Stolt family up from Illinois to the dryer plains of Ohio, during which time, Bill had witnessed all manner of calamity from floating houses to starving herds and had come to believe that traveling between the States of the Union involved passage through levels of watery Purgatory. It was also on that cross-country trip that he found a crate of books, miraculously dry and balanced on a steep rock—these were French novels translated into English, and even before he could read, they became his most important possession, talismans rescued from the rushing waters. Perhaps it was because those books came from the end of the world, he thought, that they eventually provided him with a temporary exit.

He sounded out words from the flood books for Uncle Dean as the poor man convalesced in the upstairs bedroom, left arm no longer ending in a cherry pit, but a wad of cotton gauze that sprouted blood roses on the hour like an ornate German clock. When Dean got frustrated with the boy's stops and starts, he would grab the book from Bill and read aloud. "Mr. Phileas Fogg lived, in 1872, at No. 7, Saville Row, Burlington Gardens, the house in which Sheridan died in 1814." Dean grimaced at this sentence, barely awake. "You see there, boy," he said. "There isn't anything worth reading in these. Just a bunch of details about rich people who don't even live in America."

Bill took the book from his uncle's good hand and ran a finger over the embossed cover. "This one's about a hot-air balloon that travels around the world," he said, "and this other's about a submarine."

Dean coughed. "Bring me one about good farm life and then we'll see."

His wounds went septic after a week, and he ended up throwing himself down the steep farmhouse stairs and dragging his body into the snow, which he attested felt like a bed in Heaven's finest mansion. Dean went mad from the poison in his blood, and Bill suspected that his father, in his secret heart, had appreciated the service the McCormick provided. The machine left him, after all, with half a brother but in full control of the family farm.

Bill, nearly nineteen and more savvy at farming than Dean had ever been, tried to reason with his father, saying they could repair the Case threshing machine, but the old man merely scowled over the tops of his wire-rim spectacles—blue eyes like the centers of twin gas flames. He slid one hand along the McCormick's belt, jockeying the flywheel, and said that when he was a boy they'd pounded wheat on a threshing floor using oxen. Compared to that, *any* machine, even a dangerous one, was a convenience. "By the time we fix that Case, the wheat will have rotted in its sheaves," he said. "The McCormick hurt Dean. That's the truth. But Dean wasn't watchful. My brother would have let water burn in a pot."

So the red McCormick was put into active service once again, positioned in the barnyard far enough from the chicken coop and the apple orchard where the sheep grazed to avoid frightening the animals. Bill's wife said it looked like a true instrument of terror—some medieval attempt at representing the ineffable for the purpose of a Passion play. Bill considered this observation as he worked the throttle on the engine's high platform. If God was anything like the McCormick—strung together by bailing wire and tenpenny nails—they were all in quite a corner.

His mother and father had gone to town, leaving Minarette and him to play farmer and his wife—parts that made them both uneasy. A hill of grain rose slowly in the wagon while a pile of chaff took shape in the grass, casting a low hump of shadow to one side. Bill was covered in coal soot from the steam engine's chimney pipe, and from time to time, he turned to Minarette and grinned, assuming he looked like some variety of sulfurous demon risen from the depths of Hell and knowing how she'd pretend to hate such waggishness. His teasing and her chilly responses were one of their mutually agreed-upon contrivances. They practiced their relationship even when there was no audience to watch. In reality, Bill felt heart-heavy and longed to see the black church buggy float into view, Cal in the buck seat guiding the horses with effortless twitches of his wrist. The two men would register each other in the way they used to as boys, as if some mark had been made on an invisible scoring card.

Upon catching first glimpse of Calvin Hascomb in the evening light of the county fair, Bill had felt that he was looking into some poor mirror at an image of himself, faded to such an extent that it lacked all color and weight, and perhaps because of these defects, was able to enchant. Cal had blond-white hair and pale lips. His eyes were blue in the same impossible sense that water appears blue until cupped in the hand. They were both thirteen, and Cal's family had come from Missouri after a flood similar to the one that had driven Bill's people up from Illinois. The two of them took to each other and played games of chance all evening, pitching baseballs at bowling pins and cheering each other's laughable skills. Bill finally won a tiger with shoe-polish stripes and eyes of melancholy green and gave it to Cal who carried it proudly the rest of the night.

When Bill described these scenes to Minarette, she warned him that she thought he'd been deceived. "The apprentice preacher has allowed religion to bend him in ways that no man should be bent," she said. "You don't see it, Bill, because you've know him too long. But from what you've described in your stories, I can tell you though that Calvin Hascomb, the boy, and Calvin Hascomb, the man, are two distinct substances."

She herself hailed from Chicago, and though she'd brought only a small dowry, she'd managed to drag all her expensive taste and eloquence out of the city—high-collared dresses, cloisonné broaches, and a comportment most farm girls would never dream of adopting. She seemed a piece of urbanity, transported, and her body too looked like it was derived from the delicate architecture and light that Bill had seen in postcards. To some degree, he'd married her out of spite for the fact that as soon as he'd turned eighteen, his parents had been on him, pushing him to find a girl. Not the right girl, but *any* girl as long as she knew how to work a farm. They'd nearly thrown him on poor Clara Hutchinson one Sunday at church, even though she'd had a cough since infancy and a cloudy eye. Settling down was important, his father told him. It would get him right in the Lord's eyes, and, on a more practical level, would provide progeny. "Without blood," his mother said, "a farm withers.

Family is the life of a place like this." So when he caught sight of Minarette Anderson at a barn dance, Bill saw his chance. She'd arrived that week from Chicago to visit her cousin, piquing the interest of everyone in town, and he liked the way she glared disdainfully at the farm boys in their haphazardly polished boots and checkered shirts. Bill was brave enough to ask her to dance, and after that, he hadn't let go for the rest of the night. She smelled not of lemon verbena as the other girls, but of French perfume which mixed with the smell of her vitriol and excited him. He recognized her as something new—a sophisticate that his parents would fear. Surprisingly, she'd warmed to him as well, clasping her hands behind his neck and moving to the sound of the slow German fiddle. She whispered, "I do hate all of this, Bill—these fools playing at culture."

"They don't know any better," he said, touching the stiff crinoline of her skirt. "Most of 'em haven't ventured beyond Union township."

"And you?" she asked, looking to the white carnation pinned on his vest. "You seem a man of difference."

His grin made him feel handsome in the lantern light. "The only places I've gone, ma'am, are of my own making."

"Like my father," she said, dryly, "the renowned playwright of the Chicago stage."

"I've done nothing as fine as all that," Bill replied, "unless you consider a grain silo fit for tragedy."

Minarette contemplated this. "I might prefer it to my father's stilted atrocities. How long do you think it would take to make a corn-fed Salomé of me?"

Bill did not know *Salomé* but thought Minarette looked like an oil painting fit for a museum in the farmhouse window, a *tableau vivant* with one white hand against the curtain and a beam of sunlight hooked across her powdered face. He turned from the thresher to wave again, but she did not raise her hand in response. She only stared at the strangeness of his work and sipped his mother's coffee, which she complained was as weak as tea. There was a look of perturbation on her face, and she, too, from time to time, glanced toward the road.

Minarette was no real worry to Bill. He continued to enjoy her presence and had even begun to think of her as something of a compatriot—another piece that did not fit. On top of that, she was able to occupy his parents in ways that he hadn't imagined possible; it seemed that they'd taken on their daughter-in-law as a new project, determined to translate this gadabout into a rustic girl of the farm. His mother tried to teach her how to churn butter and collect eggs from the chickens, but inevitably Minarette could not get the cream to set and broke foul smelling yolks across her stylish dresses. She would cry and sometimes even throw herself down in the tall grass of the yard. Bill's mother and father would lean over her, cooing kindnesses, worried that they'd damaged something dear. Bill wondered sometimes if she had not come to the farm for him but for his parents, born from their wish for a daughter. During their drawn-out scenes of instruction, he crossed his arms and rested against the porch post, smiling at his wife's ability to control their small universe. Once Minarette had even convinced his mother into having her face painted "city style," and the poor woman had gone around for a whole day with rouge on her doughy Dutch cheeks until she couldn't take it anymore and scrubbed herself with lye. Minarette had also used a length of ribbon to tie bells around the necks of all the sheep in the orchard—a contribution to what she called the farm's "pastoral scene." When the herd moved together, they were a choir.

Though these antics provided small pleasures, Bill felt a weight in his chest, as if an all-consuming pile of chaff, spilled from the mouths of a hundred identical Mc-Cormick threshing machines, was building. Distractions sometimes diminished that pile, but he found lately that he had to pull himself through daily work, taking no real joy in dances or fairs. Like his wife, he too was living a life he hadn't expected, but his blood was stamped all over the land, pounded into the fields, and where blood was concerned, there was little chance of escape—unless through acts of the imagination. And that variety of escape was sadly temporary.

The crate of French books he'd found during the flood were all written by a man called Jules Verne, and Bill had taken greatest enjoyment in the author's more isolating adventures like *The Steam House* and *From Earth to the Moon*. As a boy, he'd imagined himself traveling in that steam powered mansion that was moved by a mechanical elephant across foreign deserts. A desert, after all, was the opposite of a farm, dead and dry where the other was lush. He loved the idea of being carried away from everything he knew: the daily chores, the parents, and the church folk. And from those deserts of Araby, he'd traveled to the gardens of the moon in a metal oil barrel that looked enough like a rocket to take him there. The lunar gardens provided not food but strange flowers with billowing petals, stirred by a solar wind and lit with gentle phosphorescence as all things were on the moon. Bill had luxuriated in those gardens, dragging his fingers through luminous pools, climbing the stalks of roses that towered toward the stars. And until Cal had come into his life, transported by the flood waters, he'd done all of his traveling alone.

Though Cal was Bill's physical opposite, wan and white where Bill was thick and dark, he was his metaphysical compatriot, a perfect partner for playing Jules Verne. And when they'd reached the moon or their mechanical elephant had grown tired and they were stranded in the sugar-colored oceans of the desert, that is when they found themselves the happiest. Sometimes they played at being men in search of an exotic wife. Other times they were just Cal and Bill, top-notch adventurers. Bill would touch Cal's white hair, saying that if they ran out of money, they could sell such a pelt for a good price. Cal would laugh and stroke Bill's own hair in return, saying it was like crude oil, and if their rocket ship ran low, they could shave it off and pour it into the engine.

One boy seemed to illuminate the other, and nearly everyone in town remarked on the way they burned.

"It's like we don't need anything," Bill said, as they lay on the floor of the hayloft, fingertips nearly touching. Barn swallows flitted between the dark rafters, carrying bits of straw, illuminated by sunlight that leaked in through cracks in the roof.

"Need is a dangerous word," Cal replied. "The only thing any man truly *needs* is a purpose that edifies."

Bill mulled this over, wondering if his purpose might possibly be to remain in physical proximity to Cal for the rest of his life.

"Spiritual improvement," Cal continued, closing his eyes. "That's what the Reverend Fellhorne says. Every man must build a temple."

"A barn isn't good enough?" Bill asked.

Cal laughed. "No, Bill. A barn is not."

At the age of sixteen, without good warning, Cal began his studies to become a minister, working privately at the church with Revered Fellhorne, a red-faced prophet of damnation, and to Bill's dismay, the ministry seemed to cool his friend, moving Cal toward some absolute zero in which no motion or life was possible. Cal stopped working at his family farm and then stopped coming to Bill's for games. His skin took on a glassy sheen, as if transmogrified, becoming a delicate ornament that an old woman might be proud to sit on her shelf. He no longer drank root beer nor went swimming at Brook's Pond. His white-blond hair turned into a field of icy thistles, and even his liquid eyes went hard.

On the day Cal announced his intention to follow the ministerial path, they were sitting on a bale of straw near the lowing cows, and Bill was kicking his boot against Cal's, trying to knock the other boy's foot into the air. Both had grown accustomed to these sorts of physical intrusions and though they usually ended in wrestling, neither seemed to mind. Cal was carrying the family Bible, a worn object with a soft hide cover, embossed with a faded Methodist cross. Already, he had begun to wear white clothes that matched his fine skin—a living snowstorm of shirt, suspenders and trousers, even going as far as buttoning a starched collar at his neck. "Bill, have you considered why the Bible has only two testaments?" Cal asked, hefting the book. "There's the Old and the New—the book of the Father and book of the Son. But there are three members to the Trinity, isn't that right?"

Bill shrugged, not accustomed to his friend playing at rhetoric. He wanted to rest his forehead against Cal's neck which was still plain and strong because he'd only recently given up farm work, though this was an act he'd never dare attempt. "Well, I've been thinking about it," Cal continued. "It's the sort of question Reverend Fellhorne doesn't much appreciate. He says that Abraham didn't question God nor did Moses. But I think it's important to work things out before you go preaching to other people, don't you?" Cal let the Bible fall open between them. "How many pages do you see here?"

Looking down at the book, Bill was glad he was being asked to count instead of read. He had trouble with the ornamentation of King James and didn't want to embarrass himself. Reading Jules Verne was easier, not to mention more interesting. "Two pages," he answered. "Left and right, facing."

"That's how many I used to see too," Cal said. "Only recently, while listening to a sermon from the reverend about the Holy Ghost did I begin to perceive the third page." Cal touched the air between the two open Bible pages, pinching his fingers together as if holding something thin and vertical. "You have to *learn* to read the Testament of the Ghost," he went on. "It's not immediately visible, but once you gain the ability, you realize it's the most important part of the book."

Bill leaned forward, squinting. He wondered if Cal was making a metaphor or if he actually saw something there. "So what does the invisible page say?" Bill asked.

Cal grinned, the same saw-toothed expression he wore when Bill asked him to look through their tin can periscope and describe the gardens of the moon. "The Testament of the Holy Ghost doesn't say words. It's not that simple. It makes a noise like music." Then he sang a few discordant notes, loud enough to make the swallows take wing.

"All right, all right. I heard enough of that," Bill said, wincing.

"You know what the song means?" Cal asked.

Bill shook his head.

"It means I'm gonna be an important man," Cal replied. "It means I have something to say."

Without thinking, Bill grabbed the boy's pale hand, brought it to his mouth and quickly kissed it. Cal recoiled as if burned. "What was that?"

"I've heard it's what you do to important men," Bill said.

Cal did not speak again. He lay in the straw studying the back of his hand as if Bill's lips might have left a mark.

*

TWO YEARS MORE AND BILL HAD MARRIED Minarette Anderson who attested to not believing in any sort of god, a refreshing notion in farm country where everyone seemed to wear a wooden cross. It was generally agreed that Minarette's atheism was part and parcel of her city ways and therefore mysteriously accepted by most. Minarette confided to Bill that Calvin Hascomb's additions to Reverend Fellhorne's sermons gave her a bad case of the chills. "He looks like a crazy person in all those white clothes," she said one day when she and Bill were at a church picnic, watching Cal from some distance. "And when he talks about the Holy Ghost, I can't help but picture some loose-jawed ghoul hovering behind him, waiting to do his bidding. Who's ever heard of an invisible testament that sings? He'd be laughed off the pulpit in Chicago."

"It's not like that, Min," Bill said. "He's not trying to harm anyone. He's trying to *nourish* them."

"Imagination can work both ways, Bill. Nourishment or disease, and your friend is a blight, clearly indicated by those clothes. My father has a similar sickness. He transforms it not into sermons for the pulpit but hollow dialogue for the stage."

"Tell me more about those plays, why don't you," Bill said, wanting to change the subject and having heard little about Minarette's family. Only her sister and cousin had attended the wedding.

"There's very little to say," she replied. "He is as cruel to his characters as he is to me."

"What sort of cruelty?"

"A subtle kind," she said, looking toward the lake.

"Is that why you never ask to go back to the city?"

"Partly," she said. "For all its buildings, Chicago can be an empty place."

He attempted to touch her hand on the gingham blanket, but she pulled away. "I'm sorry," he said.

She attempted a smile. "Don't be. I'm just feeling cold."

Most of the time, Bill was fine with his wife's temperature. In bed, she folded her hands over her stomach and lay staring up at the ceiling like a woman in a casket. Once he'd had gotten up the courage in the dark of their bedroom to ask why she'd married him—she so clearly did not think of him as a wife thought of a husband. Minarette took her time in answering this question. In a measured voice, she said, "I married you for the same reason you married me. Because I understand that much of life is theater."

He waited for her to go on, and when she didn't, he said, "How do you mean?"

Her small chest rose and fell beneath the neatly tied bow on her nightdress. "We all choose a stage," she said. "If we choose poorly, no one comes to the show or worse yet, they bring rotten produce. People can be cruel if they do not appreciate your character, as I'm sure you're aware."

"Seems hard to believe a woman like you would come all the way out here and choose a farm as her stage."

Even in the darkness he could see her discomfort, lips parted over teeth. "I didn't choose a farm, Bill," she said. "I chose a high and distant plain. I can be a woman of finery here because people are still foolish or kind enough to believe in such things."

He shifted his weight in the bed, unsure of her meaning, then thinking about how the cook at Gardener's Kitchen served Minarette a special plate, extra nice with all the trimmings, to make her feel at home. They held bolts of fabric for her at the general store, believing it was of a quality she might have encountered in the city. Mrs. Emmet at the post walked into the street to meet them and personally deliver Minarette's exotic mail. He'd never considered that Chicago might not be the place they'd all imagined.

When he fell asleep that night, Bill found himself wandering through a city that leaked pistons and gears from its shadows. He called the names of everyone he knew until his throat went dry and his voice would no longer make a sound. Finally he leaned against a wall, exhausted and hardly believing that after all those years of yearning to leave the farm, he'd come to understand that there was nowhere else to go.

*

THE WAGON WAS HALF FULL of wheat and a great hill of chaff had accumulated behind the McCormick. Bill adjusted the throttle, listening closely to the engine for distress. He watched the road, hopeful still for Cal's wagon. He'd sent a letter into town with another farmer days ago and wrote only that he wanted to talk before Cal's leaving. He hadn't seen his friend for months except at church where the barely recognizable figure in white sat at the right hand of Reverend Fellhorne, sometimes standing to preach near the end of the service, but then disappearing behind a polished oak door before Bill could detain him. Cal no longer seemed to walk on the ground as other people did but rather floated through an invisible ether, perhaps supported by the hand of the Holy Ghost itself. Bill worried that Cal might come permanently unteathered from this town and this cluster of insignificant farms. He'd slip off into the stratosphere, as Minarette must have done when she left Chicago. But he would not let Cal go off to Toledo like that. He would have his say.

As for when exactly he'd decided on what to say, he wasn't sure, but knew it had occurred to him around the same time as Minarette's speech about life being theater. Bill understood that one way to ensure a man did not continue to devote his life to the ministry was to draw back the curtain and show him that there was, in fact, no such thing as a God. Or even if there was, He was a small and distant body, and there were more fulfilling idols here on Earth. Bill had decided to play out a scene. He wanted to take Cal into the orchard and lift an apple from a branch. He imagined the sheep mingling around them, ringing their bells as Catholic altar boys did when a host was raised. Transubstantiation—Bill had learned the word from Minarette who'd been raised Catholic because her father appreciated the grandeur of High Mass. If bread could become a body, then the apple might become a whole world. He and Cal could play out a final story together—a new creation in which there was no Fall. Instead, they would be enfolded in the garden. They could remain there, isolated. If there was no city that offered true escape, then they would invent a place as they had when they were boys. Bill understood, of course, that they were no longer children and games of the imagination could only go so far, yet he thought such a diversion might be enough to catch Cal's attention, to remind him what they had once been.

When working out exactly what to say, he'd even gone as far as asking Minarette for help, approaching her while she was busy with one of her cross-stitches which, unlike his mother's country patterns, revealed the image of some ancient temple covered in statuary. "Min," he said, dragging the tip of his boot along the seam of the floorboard, "if you were—well—if you were lacking in the adoration that you currently garner, how might you attempt to draw such attention?"

She glanced at him. "Are you trying to seduce the horses again, Bill, because that isn't going to work."

"I'm just interested. I mean, you seem to have some sort of power. Even those who are obstinate eventually fall into step."

"I practice witchcraft," she said, poking her needle through the fabric.

"Be serious, Min."

She sighed, looking at him with dark eyes. "If you want someone to care for you, Bill, you must be straightforward. Simply tell that person what you require. Be bold to the point of belligerence. You'd be surprised what people are willing to give if you simply ask for it."

"A straightforward dialogue," he said, beginning to walk away. Minarette called him back, voice softer than usual. "The question is, whose affections do you want to acquire, Bill?" When he turned, he saw she'd put her cross-stitch aside, and he found he could not answer. "Not mine," she said.

"I'm sorry." His voice was barely audible even in the silent parlor.

"No need for apologies," she replied. "We're beyond that. But asking for affection can be dangerous business. One of my father's early plays was called *All the Birds of Africa*. A mess of a drama, though it did have something to say. He didn't know the first thing about the continent, of course, and made up most of the details, using poorly digested bits of anthropology. But the general plot concerned a group of missionaries making their way down the Congo, attempting conversions at every port. They told everyone they met that God was love and that He wanted nothing more than to receive their love in return. The missionaries traveled in a houseboat painted boldly with crosses, and they sang hymns to the crocodiles. Most of their failures at conversion were caused not by their own actions but by a series of absurd accidents and intrusions. My father contrived these events to make the missionaries look like fools because he enjoyed that sort of embarrassment. These men and women, who'd begun their adventure with pride in their hearts, fell deeper and deeper into the sort of despair and lust that my father often wrote about. In the end, the missionaries agreed to set fire to their boat and surrender themselves to the whims of the Congo, knowing they might die or be swept to a place where no one knew who they were. They decided to unmake themselves because life was not worth as much as they thought. More than that, *they* were not worth as much."

"That's a grim story," Bill said. "I'd be surprised if anyone would want to see that."

"People flocked to it," Minarette replied. "They applauded loudly at the end when the actors took their bow in front of the ridiculous burning boat. There are people, Bill, who enjoy seeing things burn because that is the way they think the world should be."

"I can't say I understand that point of view."

"I know," she said. "I know you can't."

*

THE SUN HAD DIPPED toward the western field, and Bill paused for a moment at his work, allowing the McCormick to tear and cut the wheat already in its gut. He passed one hand across his brow and squinted at the road. Still there was no sign of Cal's wagon, but the moon had risen, and it seemed for a moment to act as a kind of proxy, glowing and pale like his friend, suspended by some unseen force. He did not realize Minarette had come outside until she was standing directly in front of him, holding a tin cup of water. Bill took it from her and drank, and she spoke to him, but he could barely hear her words over the cacophony—something about dinner—his parents coming home—maybe something about how she was sorry how things had worked out. She touched his arm lightly then turned away before he could question her, ascending the porch steps with the hem of her dress gathered in one hand so it did not drag. When Bill turned back to the thresher, he saw the flywheel was turning more slowly than it should have been and the engine was whining, begging for its steam to be released. In a matter of moments, the boiler began to shake and hiss, and Bill knew he needed to adjust the throttle but found that he could barely move. His legs were heavy, as were his arms. The platform atop the engine seemed miles away.

The clatter and whine of the thresher and its engine were developing a kind of rhythm—a strange music. Bill thought of the invisible Book of the Holy Ghost, the way it sang a song that only Cal could hear, and he wondered if his old friend would be able to hear the thresher singing too. He realized that if he turned toward the road at that moment, he might be able to catch a glimpse of Cal himself standing there, arms crossed and grinning as if he were still a boy. Cal wasn't coming from town. He'd been standing there all along, watching the work, watching Bill's definite and continued existence. Cal knew that the right kind of music made the invisible become visible. And now that Bill was finally ready to see—it was too late. The thresher's song was nearly through.

Of Wool

THE ATTIC SHUTTER cast a ribwork of sunlight across the surface of the rug, illuminating the figures. The longer Aubrey studied the humped and trudging things, the more he thought they might be an attempt to represent some prehistoric ancestor of the modern pig, though the amateur work of the weaver made it difficult to tell. The animals were woolly-faced with no proper snout, and instead of hooves, they had what looked like single-knuckled fingers. Their eyes were milk-white and hard like the horny tusks that protruded from their jaws, and the rug maker had glued hair to the fraying wool of their underbellies—long, decadent strands of gray that seemed to drag along the ground as the pigs followed the corded road past cottages thatched with yellow wool. In the distance stood the ruin of a once fine farmhouse. Rot had effaced the second story, and only one of a broken gable remained. A shadow protruded from its window, likely the result of an awkward knot, though Aubrey thought it also looked as if someone beneath was pressing a finger to the wool.

The world in the rug was not meant to reflect Aubrey's own. Being the grandson of Bird Heidler, he was accustomed to this sort of exclusion. "Sisal and wool, horsehair and dye," Bird had once told a darkened auditorium of graduate students, "these substances are brought together by the woman's hand to become the architecture of her invisible self. Like the spider, she is enlarged by her creation. She is rug and hearth, house and landscape." On the large screen behind Bird, an image of one of her more famous endeavors appeared—the piece Aubrey thought of as "Rug with Womb." Students shifted in their seats for a better view. The rug, woven from fisherman's rope that Bird had unbraided by hand, didn't rest on a flat plain. Instead, a shapeless cone rose from the weft, creating a sort of mouth. As a child, Aubrey thought of this rug as a place to hide, a comfortable enclosure for dreaming, but from an adult perspective, the piece seemed like maybe it wanted to be fed.

The rug Aubrey found in the attic was nothing like one of Bird's abstractions. Less refined, less intellectual—it was a *narrative* rug, but what was the story? Prehistoric pigs lay siege on an old house? He knelt in the dust, wondering if this might be one of Bird's early attempts. A failure stowed away? The whole thing stank of mordant: an acrid smelling fixative that Aubrey recognized from Bird's studio. She'd told him once that *mordant* meant "to bite"—aptly named, she'd said, because of the way the chemical fastened to woolen fibers. She'd snapped her teeth at him in good humor. Aubrey had dislodged the rug from a pile of broken boxes filled with vintage issues of *Life* magazine, all from the fifties and sixties when Bird's star was on the rise. The covers showed pastel images of the Kennedys and pho-

154

tographs of the unknown depths of outer space. Aubrey, in a T-shirt and jeans, had set out to make a catalogue of the attic's artifacts that afternoon but never expected to discover something as important as a lost rug.

He was soon to become executor of Bird's estate, his own mother lacking competence, and Bird herself growing sicker by the day. Unlike Bird's artistic force, the estate would be under Aubrey's control. He imagined interviews about his nearly symbiotic existence with his grandmother—questions concerning his understanding of her work, his notions of where she might have taken it had she not fallen ill. Some interviewer might even ask if Aubrey, too, was an artist. The answer would be a self-deprecating no. Only an assistant. He'd studied art history at Northwestern for two years before Bird had pulled him back, saying she needed his help. "It's just that things get so disorganized when you're away, Aubrey," she'd said. "I don't feel like myself without you in the house." And he'd sympathized. Bird needed him, so he returned without complaint and then took pains to convince himself that coming home had been the right choice, that the slippery seven years that followed had been productive for him. The estate was certainly worth the work, though what bothered him was never being quite sure *what* he'd given up. Camaraderie? He'd made only a handful of acquaintances at school. Education? Bird had been right. Her lessons were superior to any class. Autonomy? That was the issue with teeth. In coming home, had he somehow become a part of her? Had he been consumed?

Aubrey forced his thoughts back to the newly discovered rug. Every textile in the house had supposedly been inventoried by the representative from the Museum of Folk Art, Stanley First, who'd been chosen to curate Bird Heidler's work. Mr. First had been enthusiastic, clucking and gasping at each find. He'd disregarded Aubrey during his tour of the house, directing all pleasantry and analysis to Bird herself—once an angel of the Arts and Crafts movement, now more an angel of confusion, vacant in her parlor bed, unable to even tie the laces of her peasant boots.

Aubrey didn't feel slighted. He could, after all, understand First's fascination. Even as a remnant, Bird still engaged. Her long fingers appeared dexterous and strong, though they were no longer able to trip across the warp threads on her loom. Even her eyes, settled deep in their sockets, remained oddly sharp, as if still envisioning patterns. Stanley First wore a ring of braided silver which Bird followed with interest. "My dear Mrs. Heidler—the way you break the surface here is remarkable. What did you use? Are these *broom* bristles?"

Bird rarely answered questions, was usually *unable* to answer, though the look on her face made Aubrey wonder if her silence, in this case, was less a symptom of her illness and more a sign of succinct disrespect. She didn't like people who made a living from talking. "If you know anything about art," Bird had told him once, "you know it isn't about talk—it's about the silences."

During the initial appointments after her diagnosis, Bird's doctor had talked at length about plaques and tangles, abnormalities in her brain that would build and eventually lead to loss of memory and self. Aubrey sat with his grandmother, not holding her hand because she wouldn't allow it. Once her conscious memory was gone, the subconscious would rise and spread. Bird would experience a return of long-forgotten instances and desires, but eventually even those memories would be taken by the plaques and tangles. Aubrey couldn't help but think those words, "plaques and tangles" sounded like rug-making terms and imagined Bird's insides looking more like one of her rugs, snarled to abstraction, hung with strange ornaments and ready to burst.

He decided to take the rug with the pigs downstairs so Bird could have a look. Certain objects still triggered reactions, though most of the time, she couldn't even remember his name. He, who'd been her satellite. Even as a child, sitting on a pillow by her loom, he'd been fascinated by the rhythmic clatter and the way the shuttle cleanly pulled weft thread across the warp. His grandmother had rocked gently while she worked, glasses balanced on the tip of her nose, hair in an ashen knot. He remembered thinking that Bird was releasing the rug, that the loom was a kind of wooden bridge between her inside and her outside, a dangerous bridge that only Bird was clever enough to cross, pulling rugs behind her.

At thirty, Aubrey was nothing more than Bird's hireling, and the loom was just another object he had to dust because she didn't trust the maid. His mother had left him with Bird when he was seven, fastening the top button on his shirt and telling him that maybe he could be a rug maker one day too. He'd been generally pleased by his abandonment because it had rid him of his mother's irrational rants, her chains of cigarettes, her garish friends. She lived in Florida on the stipend Bird provided and called herself everything from a mystic to a documentary filmmaker. Once, she'd set out to make a movie about people who were trying to locate the world's navel in central Florida. The navel, the searchers claimed, was the site at which the Earth's umbilical had once been tethered to the Godhead. To touch the navel was to see the shape of Him, the outline of a body freshly moved from a bed. They never found the navel, of course, and his mother never cut her film. The shape of God, she told

Aubrey, was curiously similar to a hole the project had left in her bank account.

The sound of the rug bumping down the two flights of stairs must have drawn Bird's attention because when Aubrey arrived on the landing, she waited below, one hand clutching at a green costume necklace. He made a note to have another talk with the day nurse when she returned from lunch—to tell her that Bird wasn't some doll. He had no idea where the nurse found such awful things. Maybe she even brought them from home.

Bird was braced against the polished newel post, and there was something of an old sea captain in her wide-legged stance, though the only ocean in the foyer was her own mind—deep and corrosive, full of ruinous salt. Her white hair was frayed, uncombed, hanging almost to her shoulders.

"Could you move, Bird?" he asked, prickling at the whine in his own voice. "Please?"

In response, she pulled at the green necklace until it looked like it might break. Aubrey made himself as small as possible, pushing the rug against the railing in an attempt not to knock Bird down as he squeezed past. He allowed the heavy roll to fall on top of Bird's own foyer rug that was intentionally broken into a pile of unfinished fibers. Stanley First had been horrified to see the art there for everyone to walk on. Bird, in the old days, would have been pleased, saying, "If it doesn't provide a service, then we can't rightly call it a rug, can we?"

"I found this in the attic," Aubrey said, speaking slowly. "The man from the museum didn't see it. I was thinking it was one of yours. But then it doesn't look like anything you've ever made. Will you look?" He used his foot to unroll the rug, and the pigs appeared one by one on their road. The gables of the ruined farmhouse pricked the rotten sky. With uncharacteristic suddenness she came forward to stand on the corded road like one the pigs, another soldier in their prehistoric army. He put his hand on her hard shoulder. "Just look. Tell me if you made it."

She stared at the pigs and whispered, "Fucking old thing." The new vocabulary that had emerged from the forest of plaques and tangles still disturbed him. Bird had rarely cursed in her other life.

"I found it under some boxes," he repeated. "Stanley First didn't see it."

"The mole rat?" she asked.

"That's him," he said. "When did you make the rug, Bird?"

She touched the closest pig with one slippered foot. "Maybe I didn't make this one. I'm not the only rug maker in the world, you know."

"Who did make it then?" Aubrey asked.

She raised her faint eyebrow. "I don't know, Thomas," she said. "Some things are better left alone, aren't they?" Even before she finished the sentence, she looked as though she realized her error but didn't know how to correct it.

"It's Aubrey," he said. "You always told me I looked like your brother. Sharp features, remember? It's all right."

"Thomas is dead," she said.

"That's right."

"Fucking Thomas."

Aubrey tried to redirect, "The rug," he said. "Did you—"

"I don't know if anyone *made* it," she said.

"Of course someone did, Bird. It's here, isn't it?"

"Some things just arrive. My stomach hurts. Could you make some tea, Aubrey?"

"Do you want help getting back to bed?"

She was too interested in the nub of shadow that protruded from the gable window to look at him. "Where did you say you got it?"

"The attic."

"Where they found her," she said.

"What's that?"

Bird reached for the nub of shadow with her toe but then drew back. "Would you like to hear an old story?"

He nodded, pleased that the rug had indeed been a trigger.

"When I was young, my father kept pigs, and he let me take one out of the pen to keep as my own. A little pink girl. She ate the purple wool my mother spun. Chewed it up. And I was so angry, I chased her around the yard with a rake."

"Purple wool," Aubrey said. "That's charming."

"My little pink girl was afraid," she said. "I should have let her have the wool. What did it matter if she ate it?"

"It all turned out fine, I'm sure. It was just a pig."

Bird pulled the green necklace again. "Not just a pig," she said. "My little pink girl. The one we took walking in the evening. The one we took up to the attic room when we were secret."

He was halfway down the corridor that led to the kitchen. "*Who* was secret?"

Bird answered with a question. "Is she coming?"

"The nurse? She's at lunch. Don't worry. She won't be back to bother you for—"

"Not the nurse," Bird said. "The girl. We used to take the pink girl walking, until I married your grandfather and left the old country for good. I didn't want to leave, but that was the thing to do. Marry a soldier. Move away. She was broken. Instead of mailing regular letters, she mailed fragments, lists to show that she was broken. Places we'd gone with the pink girl. The color of my dresses. Things we'd never tried. I burned all the lists in the fireplace before your grandfather could see."

"Who is this *girl?*" Aubrey said.

Bird's eyes were like animals peering from holes. "Don't be stupid, Thomas. I'm talking about Hildred Vorst."

"I'm not Thomas," he said.

She kicked at the rug. "You're Thomas, and you told me that I *should* go with the soldier. That was the only way to stop being confused. But I wasn't *confused*." Putting one hand over her face, she made a quiet sound. "Now I'm confused. Oh, now I am. Make the tea, Aubrey. I'm sorry. I really am."

The hallway felt sharply canted, and Aubrey had to keep one hand on the wall just to reach the kitchen without stumbling. He had never heard of Hildred Vorst, but then again, Bird rarely talked about anyone from Poland who wasn't a member of her immediate family, and most of her stories usually only served the purpose of embellishing her persona. The new country, America, had always been more significant to her. America was where she'd been freed from Stalin's Ministry of Arts and Culture. Realism was no longer a requirement, and her rugs could finally open their mouths and scream. On top of that, he had not heard her speak so fluidly in months. The rug had knocked something loose.

Before filling the kettle, he went to the cabinet beneath the telephone and took out the green recipe box where Bird had meticulously catalogued a lifetime of yellowing acquaintances. Flipping through the thick index was like flipping through Bird's lost memory, and when he came to the V's, he found a card labeled *H. Vorst* in Bird's tight script. Under the name were the words *Poland/Deceased*.

No address, no telephone number. He considered taking the card into the foyer to see if it would dislodge any further memories, but then thought better of it. Why should he bring Bird more sadness? Hildred Vorst wasn't coming. The card answered that question. Instead he picked up the receiver, not thinking too much about what he was about to do. When his mother answer, her voice was slow, "Do you know what time it is, Aubrey?"

"Past noon," he said.

She cleared her throat.

"I wanted to ask you if you've ever heard of anyone named Hildred Vorst."

"Funny name," his mother said.

"Right," Aubrey said. "So you haven't heard of her?"

"Is she one of Mom's old lady friends?"

"Apparently Hildred and Bird were—I don't know—*involved* in Poland."

His mother coughed. "Involved? How many fruits are growing on our family tree, Aubrey? You all should move down to Florida. We've got plenty of—"

"Mother, that isn't helpful."

He could almost hear her smile. "You always did take after your grandmother, Aubrey. Never a free spirit like me. Both of you would rather cry about the world than live in it."

He hung up the phone, unsure why he'd made the call in the first place. His mother had never been a problem solver. He thought of Bird's Poland as the water boiled. She'd told him once that after the war countless bodies had been discovered in houses and fields, not only the bodies of soldiers but of everyday people who'd gotten lost in the terror of the attacks—people who'd starved to death or gone into basements or attics and ended their lives. There weren't enough coffins to

162

go around, and rugs became popular as burial vessels. There was an ancient tradition of weavers adorning funerary rugs with cypress trees and open eyes, the cypress for immortality, and the eyes, which often sprouted from the very branches of the trees, a way for the dead to see. "Not that the survivors had time to make special rugs after the war," Bird told him. "They rolled the bodies into any old rug they could find. A hand-worked rug is sacred—a part of the maker. I think people understood that."

When Aubrey imagined Bird's funeral, he pictured her body wrapped in a burial rug. He'd even started to consider the logistics, wondering if there was a code against burying the dead in something other than a coffin. The sharp tips of her black peasant boots would protrude from one end of the rug roll, and the gray curls of her hair would fall from the other. Bird would approve. One final reason a rug could never be called mere art.

Aubrey handed Bird her cup of chamomile, and she stared into its yellow depths for a moment before carefully pouring it onto the narrative rug at her feet. She watched as the stain spread through the sky and trickled down onto the hairy pigs. "Like piss," Bird said.

"Very much like that, yes," Aubrey replied, feeling exhausted.

"I haven't thought about her in years," Bird said.

"Hildred?" Aubrey said.

She folded her hands around the still warm cup. "How could I have ever forgotten?"

He took a breath. "In the card box, it says that Hildred Vorst passed away, Bird."

She looked annoyed. "Hildred isn't dead, Aubrey. She can never die. She went down the road and the pigs followed, you see?"

Aubrey followed the road to the ruined farm and the gabled window where the shadow protruded, as if demanding to be touched.

He read to Bird from the same book every night because the doctor said such patterns were healthy. The story was an old romance about a woman stranded; her ship broke apart during a storm. All the handsome sailors who'd traveled with her had drowned, and she was alone in the new city, haunted by the men she'd lost, and through a series of obscure incidents, she arrived at the belief that their spirits had taken possession of inanimate objects in the city. She went from place to place, collecting a candlestick, a compass, a printed scroll—believing that once she had reassembled the crew, they could sail off again.

Bird herself seemed not to hear the story. Instead she stared at the fireplace mantle which had been fitted with carved angels by Aubrey's grandfather long before Aubrey had been born. Unable to concentrate any longer, he closed the book. "Why didn't you ever tell me about Hildred?" he said.

She made no reply.

"How could you leave such a big hole? I listened to so many stories."

She didn't blink or move. Aubrey looked at Bird like she was already dead. "I know you're sick and I shouldn't talk to you like this," Aubrey said, "but I have to say that was cruel, Bird. Just—I mean, did you ever consider that you were my *friend* too. That you were the only real presence in my life?" He knew his dramatic exit from the parlor would have little effect, but he was no longer able to look at his grandmother. He'd lived his life believing that, though she excluded him intellectually, she *included* him in her emotional life. He'd led himself to believe she wasn't merely making use of him, and though she wouldn't listen to his own stories, he thought she'd told him all of hers.

The yellow stain on the pig rug had dried, and something about the pastoral had changed. He hadn't counted the pigs earlier, but looking at the rug in the evening light, he felt sure that one was missing. Bird had once explained a similar phenomenon, saying that people who looked at any patterned object for too long could develop a kind of anxiety. "The mind calls for a break," she said. "If a break can't be found, the mind creates one. Sometimes when I've been working on a rug for hours, I look back at what I've done, and it seems to me the whole thing changing, shifting like water before my eyes."

He didn't have much time to consider his pattern anxiety because as Bird had started whispering in the parlor, and though he couldn't hear the words, he heard the urgency well enough. "Bird," he called. "You okay?" Then she was no longer whispering, but shouting, and then something heavy hit the floor. Aubrey found Bird's body upended, legs and hips still on the bed, bound in the twisted sheet, torso hanging in midair and face planted firmly against the hardwood. Blood leaked from her nose onto the orange carpet that looked like a field of alien flowers. She struggled to right herself, and Aubrey realized he hadn't thought to put up the bedrail before storming off into the foyer. "Oh, Bird," he said. "Oh, God. I'm sorry." As he struggled to help her back onto the bed, he caught a glimpse of her bloodied face and realized she was terrified, not of him but of something behind him. "What happened?" he said, looking at the fireplace. His grandfather's carved angels.

He pulled the bedrail into place, making sure to latch it before hurrying off to the kitchen to call an ambulance. He pictured lines of fracture. It surprised him when he stopped, some ten feet from the phone in the kitchen, but he had an irrepressible feeling that something was beneath the antique phone stand, watching his approach. He heard a sick wheezing and couldn't stop himself from picturing the missing pig, the long gray hair of its underbelly spilling onto the kitchen tiles, its milky eyes buried in swollen flesh, its tusks of yellowed bone, strong enough to tear him.

Aubrey knew a pig had not crawled out of the rug, yet he couldn't take the five steps necessary to reach the telephone stand. Instead, he made a quick decision to use the phone in the master bedroom upstairs, backing down the hall from the kitchen until he was in the foyer again, standing on the rotten sky near the broken farmhouse. The pigs in the rug considered him with their pale eyes.

"It was just the thing to do," Bird was saying in the parlor. "I had to leave. Everyone agreed. My brother persuaded me. I didn't know what would happen to you. How could I?"

"Bird?" Aubrey said. He walked into the parlor, half-expecting to see Hildred Vorst with a bloated pig under each arm looking down at Bird with the kind of venom that only dead love could muster, but there was no one in the parlor except for Bird. She'd bled all over her bedding and was twisting two ends of the damp sheet with her long fingers as if she intended to weave them. "I wish that I'd stayed," she said to the empty air. "I wished it every day for a long time. I heard how they found you. All alone in the attic with the pigs."

"Bird, stop," Aubrey said.

She grabbed the novel on the bedside table and hurled it at him, then tipped the table itself onto the floor, spilling pills across the field of blossoms that were already wet with her blood. "Let me out of this bed, Thomas!" she yelled.

Aubrey found himself shaking.

"Where did you get that fucking rug?" Bird screamed.

"The attic," he said. "It's been up there all along. You forgot it."

She spat. "It's a funeral rug. You took it from the ground, from her. Now let me out. Let me see."

He disengaged the latch, let the bedrail fall. Bird watched him with hatred in her eyes, still thinking he was Thomas perhaps, or maybe realizing he was Aubrey. He backed away and watched her work her way out of the bed, this time dropping all the way to the floor, landing on her hip. She hissed in pain but kept moving. Aubrey didn't try to help, only watched as she crawled like some animal in a nightgown. When she reached the narrative rug, she pulled one edge of it across her body, covering herself with it as if the rug were a shroud. "Oh, where did this come from?" she said. "How could this be?"

Aubrey watched as his grandmother turned inside the rug, rolling herself, becoming humped and indistinct. Finally, she rested, lying utterly still.

Egyptomania

THE POET'S STUDY WAS CLUTTERED with his wife's Egyptian marvels—the plaster head of Isis, a letter opener shaped like the claw of the cat god Bast, even a shard from an actual Canopic jar that he was to use as a paperweight. Robert Southey employed his gift of afterdinner irony to downplay these knickknacks and amuse the Keswick intellectuals who gathered every Thursday at his house to sip cognac from wide-bottomed glasses and exchange observations on the state of the sovereignty. Egypt, for these thinking men, was little more than fleeting fashion—a confluence of sand and surfaces dredged up by Napoleon's recent affairs in Africa, which had little apparent effect other than to drive their wives into a mad flurry of redecoration. Never mind the vanity of the conqueror—he'd become more an arbiter of style than politics—and never mind the Marmelukes with their strange customs. What meaning could such things hold for poets and philosophers? "Tell us about your bears instead, Robert!" one of the men shouted, as another gagged on his drink.

It was well known that Southey, England's laureate, was in the process of writing a children's story about a blond girl who, upon becoming lost in the woods, came across a thatched cottage that belonged to a group of bears living like Yorkshire peasants. "Do they chew the girl up or bore her to death with Christian homilies?" asked the man. The room chuckled at the joke, and Southey attempted geniality, but such woods were rooted deep in his heart, and the girl who walked there was no subject for humor. He glanced at his wife's newly purchased earthen bowl, a replica from the Middle Kingdom. She'd placed a single carnation in it, and Southey plucked the flower, bringing it absently to his nose.

There is a painting that hangs in the National Gallery depicting Napoleon in a similar state of melancholy. After his successful defeat of the Marmelukes and his taking of Egypt, the conqueror supposedly posed on the shadowed throne of the king's chamber—a small man in a grand chair—the ceiling of the pyramid pressing down around him like a faded circus tent. Napoleon displayed the pharaoh's staff across one knee, holding it gingerly as if it might crack, and though we cannot peer into the Emperor's mind at that moment (nor Robert Southey's at the moment of lifting the flower) we can wonder at his sadness, his countenance of want. Did Napoleon imagine that soon the daughters of France and England would be wearing crocodile earrings with dangling tails or that, due to his conquest, scarab beetles would become *de rigueur*? The creature, still alive when the jeweler attached it to a woman's garments via a tiny post and chain, would be worn for the evening as a kind of living broach, a struggling conversation piece, carapace encrusted with jewels.

Sphinx sofas appeared in European homes, calling for the sitter to be cradled between their monstrous wings. It was difficult to imagine that only a few years prior, sofas did not have faces or even skulls. There were no hearts buried in the stuffing, no riddles carved in the cherry work. The sofas were featured in the so-called "Egypt rooms" of fashionable houses, hunched between fluted columns, brushed by overhanging fronds. A sun-dappled vase painted with untranslatable stiff-limbed figures often stood adjacent.

Even Robert Southey himself eventually relented to the concept of the Egypt room—largely due to pressure from his wife, Edith Fricker—purchasing not only a Sphinx sofa but also a writing desk made from the etched stone back of a jackal god. He found it difficult to dismiss the larger furnishings with humor and eventually stopped inviting the intelligentsia for Thursday dinners, using that time instead to sit at his Egyptian writing desk and pen his story of the fair-haired girl and her bears. "Edith," he said to his wife as she adjusted miniature obelisks on their mantle, "what do you think three bears would make of a young English girl if they had never seen a girl child before?"

Edith Fricker paused at her work, considering her husband's ridiculous question. He was a laureate, after all, and such notions had to be tolerated. "What color is the girl's hair?" she asked, in a tone not unlike the one she used when speaking to their young son, Hammond.

"Blond," Southey said. "Golden, actually."

"That will never do, Robert," she replied. "You must make it darker, so as not to startle the bears."

Later that night, Southey was moved not to darken the girl's hair, but to change its color from gold to silver.

Gold was average and relatable. Silver, on the other hand, seemed beatific. The girl became a saint lost among the pines, wandering among the objects of the provincial home, and certainly not even bears would harm a young saint. Like Napoleon, Silverlocks sat in chairs too large for her—thrones made for hips and fur. She too felt a deepening sadness and a sense of questioning. Why had she bothered with this dangerous investigation at all? What good did she think would come of entering the animals' house?

The *Times* reported that Napoleon had mummies dragged up from the plains of the Nile, great piles of them, to be sold to the medical community at high prices and ground into bitumen, a carbonic powder that was then mixed with oils. A mummy, when correctly prepared, became a dark and fragrant syrup, served as medicine on a plate or in a small bowl, eaten with a miniature spoon. Its bitterness was difficult to stomach and the idea of eating the dead was downright ghoulish, yet the restorative properties of the syrup were said to be worth the pathos.

Alice St. Germaine wrote in her monthly women's column, to which Edith Fricker subscribed, that she had never felt so energized as she did after imbibing the bitumen of an Egyptian mummy. "What wonderful things those ancients must have known!" St. Germaine effused. "We ourselves do not have such forethought to turn our corpses into storehouses of health and provide the same solid insurance for our children." After eating bitumen, she said she could practically feel the coolness of the Egyptian fronds on her brow, and attested to a new understanding of the sun. It was no mere ball of gas. The Egyptians had it right. The sun was an eye. The sun could *see*.

St. Germaine's column caused a flurry of correspondence from women all over England who were also enjoying the virtues of bitumen. One such reader wrote that her own flesh had developed curative properties. She'd recently revived several houseplants from near death simply by touching their leaves. And when the family dog grew sick, she'd held it against her stomach for an hour until the animal was fit again.

There were darker letters too, left unpublished, of course—a woman whose use of bitumen caused her to walk nightly and allowed her very spirit to drift into the bodies of her countrymen. Consciousness was no longer secure within her frame. She wrote that she crept like sand along the streets and among the people. She called her state Bituminoid Madness, saying she became a shopkeeper, a vagabond, even the awful man who watched girls pass through the square with their mothers. The poor woman couldn't help herself. Bitumen had opened her up, and no matter how hard she tried, she could not close herself off again.

One wonders if Robert Southey was influenced by these stories when imagining the porridge of the bears. Did he picture bowls of black bitumen for his Silverlocks to eat? Certainly those long-muzzled owners of the house didn't eat the bland pottage of England but rather a more grotesque variety, and after a meal of such strange porridge, should we be surprised that Silverlocks found herself drifting toward the staircase in a state of semiconsciousness? The girl was dreaming of the great hairy beds in the second-floor rooms, no longer concerned about the monstrous family's lumbering return. Her priceless saintly locks were tipped in the black salt of mummies, and her lips were streaked with more of the same as she ascended the staircase, the soles of her black patent shoes never quite falling on the wooden steps.

There are numerous other stories of Egyptian influence. Some went so far as to say that the Marmelukes were waging a secret war on Europe as punishment for Napoleon's pillaging. But the story that most concerns this record is what befell the Southey family not so long after the poet's humorous and disparaging statements to the men of Keswick about Egyptian revival furnishing. Southey's wife, Edith Fricker, continued to accumulate decorative pieces from the Middle Kingdom, finally purchasing an actual sarcophagus that had, until recently, housed the mummy of a little-known aristocrat. She had the piece installed in the parlor, telling the poet that she didn't find the object morbid in the least. She quoted Alice St. Germaine: "For the Egyptians, my dear," she said, stroking the poet's hair with her abbreviated fingers, "death was another kind of life."

Hearing his mother and father talk this way drew the attention of the Southey's five-year-old son, Hammond, who became curious about the new sarcophagus and one afternoon attempted to seal himself inside the box. He was too weak to move the heavy lid, so rather than experiencing full-body entombment, the boy settled for a half-death, lying in the gut of the cool stone and staring at the parlor's painted ceiling. He allowed his gaze to drift and his limbs to fall. The boy discovered the sarcophagus was more comfortable than it appeared. Stone could feel rather like a feather bed, and soon he was asleep.

When Southey returned to discover his son so pink with life in the sepulcher, he could neither speak nor move. His wife had been wrong about the Egyptian coffin. Death was death, no matter how one dressed it, and he couldn't help but picture his own father and then his grandfather, faces lit with funeral rouge. He thought of his mother who had not waited for his carriage to arrive. He'd found her impossibly lifeless in her bed.

Egyptomania

The poet's suffering did not abate when he gently lifted his son's warm body from the sarcophagus and rested the boy's head against his breast. The feeling extended into the following day when reports arrived that Napoleon had finally returned from Africa. "Tired of the dust," he said. "Sick of all the useless relics." And Southey sent word to his wife that the sarcophagus must be removed from the parlor along with all the other Egyptian trash. He instructed her to have it put behind the house where no one could see, or better yet, to have it interred. She relented. He was the laureate, after all. And so it was that a whole host of Egyptian artifacts were piled begrudgingly into a sarcophagus and buried in one of the finer gardens of Keswick, and even still, our poet was haunted by fashion.

We cannot be certain when Southey sat down to finish his story of Silverlocks, but we imagine him in the dark of the evening, an oil lamp burning on his French writing desk which had been restored to the study, replacing the one that was buried in the yard.

His wife and son are sleeping. Napoleon is once again safely ensconced at Fontainebleau. And, despite the poet's attempts to bar their way, the animal-headed gods of Egypt are moving toward their cottage again, shaking pines as they pass by on massive legs. The gods learned long ago to decorate their homes with European artifice. They find pleasure in the rustic furnishings and sensible fireplaces. They festoon their tables with tatted lace and unostentatious bowls of fruit. And what do they find sleeping in their bed? What have their predilections drawn? She with her silver face, hard and bright as a funeral mask, and her hair, a silent ivory dome.

Acknowledgments

Thanks to the editors of the publications in which the following stories first appeared:

Arts and Letters: "A Memory of His Rising";
Ascent: "Of Wool";
Conjunctions: "The Automatic Garden";
The Greensboro Review: "Fall, Orpheum";
Quarterly West: "Beneath Us";
StoryQuarterly: "A Man of History";
Third Coast: "There Are No Bodies Such as This;
Web Conjunctions: "Egyptomania."

For their editorial assistance and general encouragement, I'd like to thank Brian Leung, David Lazar, Jennie Fauls, Scott Blindauer, Greg Miller, Elizabeth and Sarah Wehri, Garnett Kilberg Cohen, Paula Payton Gurrie and Cora Jacobs. I would like to thank my mother and father for their constant kindness and support, and Chris Breier for his thoughts and affection.

About the Author

Adam McOmber is the Assistant Director of Creative Non-fiction at Columbia College Chicago where he teaches both creative nonfiction and mythology. He is also the associate editor of the literary magazine *Hotel Amerika*. His work has been recently published in *Conjunctions*, *StoryQuarterly*, *Third Coast*, *The Greensboro Review*, *Arts & Letters*, *Ascent*, *North Atlantic Review*, and *Web Conjunctions*. Currently, he is at work on a novel.

BOA Editions, Ltd.
American Reader Series

Colophon

This New and Poisonous Air, stories by Adam McOmber, is set in ITC Veljovic, a digital font designed by Jovica Veljovic (1954–), which displays a crisp precision, as if the letters were cut in stone rather than drawn with pen and ink. The display type is IllegalEdding.

The publication of this book is made possible, in part, by the special support of the following individuals:

Anonymous
Joseph Belluck, *in honor of* Bernadette Catalana
Peter & Karen Conners
Pete & Bev French
Anne Germanacos
Janice N. Harrington & Robert Dale Parker
X. J. Kennedy
Jack & Gail Langerak
Rosemary & Lew Lloyd
Boo Poulin
Deborah Ronnen & Sherman Levey
Steven O. Russell & Phyllis Rifkin-Russell
Glenn & Helen William
Ellen & David Wallack